# Jacob Michaels Is Dead

## A Point Worth LGBTQ+ Paranormal Romance

## Book 6

Chase Connor

Chase Connor Books

The Lion Fish Press

www.chaseconnor.com

www.thelionfishpress.com

To the extent that the image or images on the cover of this book depict a person or persons, such person or persons are merely models, and are not intended to portray any character or characters feature in the book.

Cover models are not intended to illustrate specific people and the content does not refer to models' actual acts, identity, history, beliefs or behavior. No characters depicted in this ebook are intended to represent real people. Models are used for illustrative purposes only.

**Book Cover Designed By: @DeanColeWriter**

CHASE CONNOR BOOKS are published by

The Lion Fish Press
539 W. Commerce St #227
Dallas, TX 75208

**© Copyright 2019 by Chase Connor**

All rights reserved. Without limiting the rights under copyright reserved above, no part of this publication may be reproduced, stored in or introduced into a retrieval system, or transmitted, in any form, or by any means (electronic, mechanical, photocopying, recording or otherwise), without the prior written permission of the copyright owner.

AUTHORS' NOTE:
This is a work of fiction. Names, characters, places, and incidents either are the product of the authors' imagination or are used fictitiously, and any resemblance to actual persons, living or dead, business establishments, events, or locales is entirely coincidental. Point Worth is a fictional Ohio town. None of this is real.

Ebook ISBN – 978-1-951860-03-5
Paperback ISBN – 978-1-951860-04-2

***To crazy ideas and the stupidity to try them.***

**And:**

*As always*:

To my beta-readers and "feedback crew": I am so glad you are all here. And I am so glad you are all so blunt with me—even if I do what I want most of the time.

To all of the readers: It has been quite a journey. I've loved every second of it. Let's get to the end together, shall we?

# Also by Chase Connor

*Just a Dumb Surfer Dude: A Gay Coming-of-Age Tale*
*Just a Dumb Surfer Dude 2: For the Love of Logan*
*Just a Dumb Surfer Dude 3: Summer Hearts*
*Gavin's Big Gay Checklist*
*A Surplus of Light*
*The Guy Gets Teddy*
*GINJUH*
*A Tremendous Amount of Normal*
*The Gravity of Nothing*
*Between Enzo & the Universe*

**A Point Worth LGBTQ Paranormal Romances**
*Jacob Michaels Is Tired (Book 1)*
*Jacob Michaels Is Not Crazy (Book 2)*
*Jacob Michaels Is Not Jacob Michaels (Book 3)*
*Jacob Michaels Is Not Here (Book 4)*
*Jacob Michaels Is Trouble (Book 5)*
*CARNAVAL (A Point Worth LGBTQ Paranormal Romance Story)*
*Jacob Michaels Is Dead (Book 6)*

**Erotica**
*Bully*

**Audiobooks**

*A Surplus of Light (Narrated by Brian Lore Evans)*

# Jacob Michaels Is Dead

A Point Worth LGBTQ Paranormal Romance

Book 6

# Table of Contents

# Point Worth, OH 1975

*Sitting atop the tree stump just inside the halo of light cast by the campfire, the man slowly opened the book, letting it come to rest upon his lap. The children gathered around the perimeter of the campfire sat in the lotus position, leaning forward expectantly. All of their parents had brought them to the old lands out by the lake to hear this story, just as parents had been doing for many generations past. Flames from the fire licked high into the night air, sending sparks and embers floating into the velvety blackness above. Skeletal arms and fingers of the trees in their deep autumn slumber flickered in and out of sight with each spout of flame from the fire. The man looked slowly around the circle of children sternly, solemnly, before suddenly clearing his throat, making the children twitch anxiously. Looking down at the book, his mouth opened, and his grave voice poured forth:*

*"Once upon a time..."*

*evil came to this land.*

*Its name...was Bloody Bones. Though, what it was, no one knows.*

*Where it came from, no one knows.*

*What it looks like, no one knows.*

*What is known is that it has almost always been here. Lurking. Waiting. Watching. From beneath us.*

*Rising from the depths of the water, it would drag wicked children into the depths, never to be seen again.*

*"Sass your parents...Bloody Bones will getcha!"*

*"If you don't clean up your mess...Bloody Bones will getcha!"*

*"Fight with your brothers and sisters...Bloody Bones will getcha!"*

*Parents would often say these things to their children, warning them that bad behavior would summon it. Bloody Bones would come for the wicked children. No one knew why everyone thought Bloody Bones only came for wicked children because, truth be told, he comes for all. Eventually, Bloody Bones comes for all of the wicked people, children and adults alike. No one is safe from it. It is everywhere at all times, waiting for its next wicked soul to claim. Though, no one really knows much else.*

*The one thing that is known is why it is here.*

*Many years ago...centuries...eons...who knows, really? Bloody Bones simply rose from the ground, given life by the very magic that permeates every inch of this Earth. But it wasn't just the magic of the land that gave life to it...it was also the evil that seems to fill the nooks and crannies where magic doesn't reach. Where there is good, there is always evil. You can't have one without the other. There must be balance.*

*Bloody Bones began its wrath of terror, claiming souls for its own. Ripping children from their beds and dragging them away, leaving tearful mummies and daddies wondering where their babes had gone. It killed livestock and family pets. Flying through the countryside, distorting the very magic which had begat it, attempting to create a new world in its vision.*

*Hell on Earth.*

*And if Bloody Bones had its way, that's precisely where we would be now. Instead of sitting around this campfire, safe and sound.*

*For many years...generations really...the people of this land lived in fear of and in servitude to Bloody Bones. Afraid to anger the master of the magic of this land. Parents clutched their children tightly to their bosoms as they put them to bed each night, wondering if Bloody Bones would come. Food and drink, sometimes pets and livestock, were left as offerings on the doorsteps of the homes as the sun went to meet the horizon each night.*

*Bloody Bones was satisfied...for a time.*

*It had magic.*

*Rule of this land.*

*Blood. Meat. Drink.*

*It was king.*

*But even kings grow weary and dissatisfied with their kingdom.*

*Bloody Bones wanted more.*

*More children were taken. More livestock destroyed. Houses were burned with families inside. His wolves terrorized the villages. Years of famine and illness cast a dark shadow over these lands. Bloody Bones cast these lands in darkness for many years.*

*But...as things usually go...where there is magic, there is hope.*

*Just as Bloody Bones appeared, so did The Guardian and The Oracle.*

*And, finally...The Witch.*

*The Witch knew that no one but she could release her people from bondage—to free them from Bloody Bones' reign of terror. Barely more than a child, the witch and Bloody Bones met on the field of battle. It was brutal, and it was not quick. The Guardian and The Oracle watched—as guardians and oracles often do—as Bloody Bones was sealed in the ground. Right here. Beneath us. Right where we sit at this moment.*

*It was obvious, as the witch collapsed to the ground, that the child might recover. However, instead of living to fight another day, the witch gave her life, the last of her power, to seal Bloody Bones away for good. As her blood spilled upon the Earth, she cast a wide net of magic with her final breath. As long as the magic of her family was in this land undisturbed, Bloody Bones would never return. It would stay sealed beneath us…forever.*

*Watching.*

*Waiting.*

*Plotting.*

*The Oracle and The Guardian watched as the land swallowed The Witch's body. A peculiar artifact sprouting from where she had laid.*

*They knew that with her spell, the witch had balanced the fate of these lands upon a razor's edge.*

*The magic would hold Bloody Bones.*

*But there are those who would seek magic.*

*To claim it as their own.*

*To use it.*

*Even the witch's own family.*

*History becomes stories, and stories become legends, and legends become myth…and myths become nothing more than lies. Future generations of the witch's family would not believe that the magic truly held Bloody Bones within the Earth. They would attempt to use the magic as it suited them, to bring them their hearts' desires. Eventually, the magic that held Bloody Bones would be gone, squandered and perverted by the very people the witch had given her life to protect.*

*With a blood oath, The Oracle and The Guardian swore to watch over these lands, to ensure that if Bloody Bones were ever to return, they would be ready. They would find the most powerful witch in the family's bloodline, and—regardless the cost—get that witch to imprison Bloody Bones again.*

*With each witch's death over the eons—oh, yes, humans are weak and seek out the use of magic, and evil never rests—Bloody Bones grew stronger and stronger. The Oracle and The Guardian knew that...eventually...Bloody Bones would soon be too powerful for the same magics to keep it at bay. One day, it would rise from these lands a final time, no matter who stood against it, and Hell would come to Earth.*

*But...then, another witch was born.*

*And The Guardian and The Oracle recognized an opportunity to be rid of Bloody Bones forever...*

"That's not true!" The boy doubled over with laughter, his arms slung across his tummy.

"True as we're sitting here!" The man's brow furrowed as he turned to glare at the boy who had distracted him from his storytelling.

"What a bunch of crap." Another kid, freshly in her teens, rolled her eyes as she jumped up from the ground. "You're crazy."

The man shrugged his shoulders as the children rose from the ground around the campfire. Chilly autumn air blew through their circle, making the firelight dance. Winter would come to Point Worth soon.

*"You'll think crazy when Bloody Bones visits you tonight." The man cautioned her, pointing his finger brusquely at each of the kids in turn.*

*Mumbling about the "crazy man" and laughing amongst themselves, the children began to disperse, heading back up to the Old House, where their parents were waiting to drive them home. Every year, on the same day, the children of Point Worth came to these lands to hear the tale of Bloody Bones. At first, this was a sacred event, regarded with great solemnity by the children who were dropped off by their parents. Over the years, it became nothing more than one of the "crazy men" in town trying to scare the children with an ancient myth about their hometown, and, before that, the lands that belonged to the indigenous peoples.*

*The man sighed to himself as he closed the book and placed his hands on his knees, preparing to rise from the tree stump, when a child caught his eye. One of the younger boys had stayed seated by the campfire, watching the man. This boy lived on these lands with his family. Curious that he would be the only child not to heckle the man or his story. The man settled back on the tree stump, his eyes turning to the young boy, sitting there by the fire, captivated and terrified, his wide eyes affixed to the man.*

*"It's just a story." The man said.*

*It had been for the sake of the boy's comfort. No truth laced those words.*

*"Where did you hear that story?" The boy asked.*

*"Same as you." The man winked. "From an old man around a campfire. The last man to own this book."*

*"Is...is it tuh-true?"*

*"Don't let it bother ya' none." The man winked at the boy. "Bloody Bones ain't comin' for you, Robert. And, if he does, I'll fight him off for ya'."*

*Robert thought about this for a moment, and then a brilliant smile split his face. Leaping up, he gave the man a wave, and then he was running back towards his family home in the clearing in the woods, away from the shores of Lake Erie. The man watched as Robert ran gleefully towards home, allowing a passing smile to adorn his face. When the boy was swallowed up by the darkness and shadows of the woods, the man's smile disappeared, and his eyes went to the fire. Shadows danced all around him as the flames licked towards the canopy of trees overhead.*

*"Ya' know," The man started at the sound of a woman's voice, "no one really believes that story anymore. Which is a problem."*

*"Who's there?" The man's head whipped around, looking for the sound of the voice.*

*"The ground can be shakin', and the wolves can be prowlin'. The moon can turn to blood, and the lake can boil…but that story is no more than a myth anymore."*

*"Who's there?" The man repeated, clutching the book to his chest.*

*His eyes landed on the spot where little Robert Wagner, Jr. had been swallowed up by the shadows. A woman, old in visage but spry in body, stepped out into the light of the campfire. The man's eyes grew as the woman, a stranger to him, sauntered out of the shadows and towards the campfire, coming to stand on the other side of the flickering flames.*

*"Where'd you come from?" The man asked, unnerved by the sudden appearance of the woman he had never seen before.*

*"Here and there." The matronly woman shrugged as she peered into the man's sparkling eyes, not yet dulled by age. "Mostly here."*

*"Who are you?"*

*The corner of the woman's mouth turned upward slightly as her eyes lingered on the man's a moment longer. Then her eyes were on the book.*

*"That book doesn't belong to you." She said.*

*With a flick of the woman's hand, the book flew from the man's grasp into the waiting, outstretched hand of the woman. She smiled at the man and promptly tucked the book under her arm. Without another word, she turned and began to step away from the campfire.*

*"Huh-who are you?" The man demanded, rising from the tree stump.*

*"Well," The woman turned back to the man, "I'm Esther Jean Wagner. Or I will be. After a spell."*

*She winked.*

*Horrified, the man jabbed a shaky finger in her direction.*

*"You aren't Esther Jean Wagner." He demanded. "Esther Jean Wagner died in childbirth years ago."*

*Esther Jean Wagner smiled.*

*"What people don't know won't hurt 'em none." She winked again. "It's amazin' what people will believe with a little magic, ain't it?"*

*"What?"*

*For a few moments longer, the woman stared at the man. Suddenly, the man lowered himself to the tree stump again, his eyes slowly moving to the flickering flames of the fire.*

*"Esther...Jean...Wagner."*

*"That's right." The woman nodded. "That's who I am. You're good about tellin' stories. Tell anyone you want about me if it suits you fine."*

*The man's head nodded up and down like a balloon on a stick.*

*"But you ain't never heard this story before." She shook the book at the mesmerized man. "That's one story you can stop tellin'. We don't need you goin' around, spoilin' the endin'."*

*"Why?" The man asked robotically, his eyes still on the fire.*

*"These kids ain't the only folks listenin'." Esther Jean Wagner's brow furrowed as the ground rumbled underfoot for the briefest of moments. "Tellin' stories is dangerous, Jackson Barkley. Some things are best left to be forgotten. For as long as they can."*

*"Why?"*

*Esther Jean Wagner's eyes moved from the ground to the canopy of skeletal tree limbs overhead. The chilly autumn breeze blew through the woods once more, ruffling her hair and threatening to extinguish the fire.*

*"It might already be too late." She said, mostly to herself, before turning her eyes to Jackson Barkley. "He's comin'. I don't doubt that you'll meet him."*

*And, with that, Esther Jean Wagner disappeared back into the shadows, the book of stories tucked under her arm. Jackson Barkley sat before the fire, staring into its slowly dying flames.*

# Chapter 1

The ground was still shaking, maybe not as bad as it had been, but cracks had formed in the ground of the parking lot outside of the football stadium.

A pack of werewolves stood in a semi-circle, their leader at the center, a smirk on his face as the woman approached. Ancient and wise, confidence announced her arrival like perfume that had been applied far too liberally. Jason and his pack sneered and smirked, attempting to look menacing as the woman walked towards their half-circle of terror. Still the ground wasn't the only thing shaking. At least, it wasn't the reason that more than one werewolf's knees were wobbly. Whether something such as a werewolf would admit such a thing, every person in the pack knew that this woman was not to be trifled with, nor was she to be treated as harmless. With the snap of her fingers, she could easily incinerate any one—or all—of them.

Jason stepped forward as the woman stepped out of the dust and shadows, approaching the pack of werewolves as though they were bunny rabbits. She had nothing to fear from the wolves that comprised the pack, whether they were in wolf or human form. If it weren't the pack, one would think that the ground shaking underfoot would have unnerved the woman, yet it did not. She was unbothered by neither the werewolves nor the quaking underfoot. After all, this was the reason she existed. She had nothing to fear, for her destiny was tied to this moment. Just like it had been to every similar event spanning back to nearly the dawn of human existence.

Jason did his best to swallow down the lump in his throat and continue to smirk at the woman at the same time, though he knew that his fear would be palpable to her. Nearly anyone would fear this woman almost as much as they would the man in the black hooded cloak. Of course, no one was certain why such a seemingly harmless creature could be nearly as fearsome as the cloaked man, yet the fear was there. Perhaps it was because she had nothing to lose or gain, regardless of how events unfurled. Maybe it was because she had no fear herself. Or maybe it was because she was able to walk along on the shifting ground in a pair of high heels and not miss a step.

"Well," Carlita popped her tongue against the roof of her mouth as she stopped a few yards in front of Jason, "I guess today is as good as any other day for an apocalypse."

"You can't do anything now." Jason attempted a snarl, but to his chagrin, it came out as a wolf-y whimper.

Carlita looked across the expanse between them with a simple smile affixed to her face.

"As if I would." She said.

Jason nodded shakily.

"My allegiances have not changed, wolf," Carlita said, holding a hand up to examine her nails lazily. "Yet, I am quite surprised that we are seeing each other so soon."

"That's *her* fault." Jason spat.

Nearly a quarter of a million miles above them, the moon shone down, full and orange.

Soon, it would be blood red, though darkness would mask it. Carlita glanced skyward and let her manicured hand fall to her side as she took in the hue of the moon, trying to mentally calculate how much longer they had. Suddenly, the ground stopped shifting. With a smile, her eyes landed upon Jason once again.

"They're no longer in Point Worth." She said. "For now."

Jason opened his mouth to speak, but a woman's voice came to Carlita's ears instead.

"They high-tailed it out of here, ya' bitch."

Carlita's smile widened as she turned her head to peer into the darkness at her right. Out of the shadows, Esther Jean Wagner stomped towards her. Clad in blue denim bib overalls, a plaid long-sleeve shirt, and gardening clogs, she looked as happy as she usually did, which was to say: *not at all.*

"Vieja loca blanca." Carlita snorted.

"Don't you talk that Spanish shit to me, Carlita." Esther Jean continued her march towards the woman in the red high heels. "You got somethin' to say, say it in a language I understand."

Jason took the opportunity to step back, slipping into the ranks of his pack, making himself a less likely target. At least a harder to hit target. Whether he would be a target for fire, a tongue lashing, or worse, he wasn't sure. He just knew that he did not want to be between the two women if they decided that they wanted to fight. It was unlikely that Carlita would allow violence to erupt during one of their meetings. Still, Esther Jean Wagner was a force all her own. She wasn't afraid of the woman in the red high heels. She had no reason to be.

"You crazy old white bitch." Carlita bobbed her head back and forth with a sneer as she took in the old woman who stopped merely a yard away. "That's not exactly what I said, Esther Jean. I added the 'bitch' because it felt right."

"How dare you talk to me like that?" Esther Jean's voice boomed.

A pack of werewolves, though in human form, cowered and whimpered. Destruction was upon them all. Whether it would come from these two women or the force that had caused the ground to shake, they weren't sure. But destruction was imminent.

"I wouldn't be talking to you at all right now if you had gotten Rob out of Point Worth sooner." Carlita examined her nails again. "Yet again, you just couldn't do your damn job."

"I did my job." Esther Jean snapped. "I got him out of this damn town before he came of age, didn't I?"

"And you did such a marvelous job."

"You look here, you bitch—"

Jason and his pack began to back up, thoughts of slinking away into the darkness crossing all of their minds.

"Don't even think about it, you sonsofbitches!" Esther Jean turned her head to snap at them.

The wolves froze in place. Carlita smiled, amused, though her eyes never left Esther Jean.

"I got him raised. I got him out of Point Worth when he was sixteen." Esther Jean jabbed a finger at Carlita's face, though she was smart enough to stay out of her reach. "I made him think everything was his own damn idea. I gave him those memories. I did everything we agreed upon. I. Did. My. Damn. Job."

"You," Carlita leaned forward, "did it poorly."

"Fuck you."

"Classy." Carlita moved back, her arms coming to rest over her chest. "You always were such a delight, Esther Jean. Oh, how I've cherished our millennia together. I'm kind of sad to see our time come to an end, even though it will mean never having to look at your face ever again."

"I did my job, damnit!"

"If you did your job, he wouldn't have come back."

"How the fuck was I supposed to know everything I did wouldn't be good enough to keep him away longer?" Esther Jean waggled her head at Carlita.

"Because I told you."

"You're always runnin' your damn mouth about something."

"That's what oracles do." Carlita turned her head to the wolves, who were, once again, trying to inch away. "If you boys don't stop being pesky, momma's gonna get mad."

Jason and his wolves flinched at the toothy smile Carlita flashed.

"Let 'em run." Esther Jean threw her hands in the air. "Where the hell are they gonna go anyway? I'm assuming they're goin' to turn tail whatever happens. Now that the arrival of their master is inevitable."

Carlita gave the wolves a stern look, then turned back to Esther Jean, all smiles once again.

"He took Lucas with him," Carlita said simply.

"Well, who the fuck saw that comin'? That was me. Some goddamn oracle you are! I told y'all pushin' them two together was gonna cause problems. I told y'all this whole goddamn plan was a bunch of cat turds hot-glued together, ya' old bitch."

"At least I've aged well." Carlita shrugged sweetly.

Esther Jean glowered at her.

"Meanness does nothing for the complexion, my dear." Carlita reached out as if to touch Esther Jean's cheek.

Her hand was slapped away sharply. Carlita shrugged again and crossed her arms over her chest once more.

"Look here." Esther Jean snarled, her finger jabbing at Carlita's face again. "I did what I was supposed to do. He left. It ain't my fault he came back. I acted put out just enough to not let on, but I never forced him to come back here. But even when he came back, I did all I could to confuse him, to make him think he was crazy, to scare him, to make him hate me. I pushed him and Lucas together again like we planned. I set him up on a date with a goddamn werewolf."

"I told him that werewolf was nothing more than a harmless pervert so he'd go on the date," Carlita interjected, unhappy with not getting her share of the credit.

"And I set up the whole scene the day after with Andrew. Hell," Esther Jean Wagner ignored her, "I had his ass jumpin' in the damn freezing lake to save a ghost. We got the werewolves after him—got assface over there to send three wolves out to the house to scare him. Even lured his ass outside in the middle of the night to be scared."

"You got Katie killed." Jason spat angrily before realizing who he was growling at, then corrected himself and calmed down.

"I got him interested in the cellar." Esther Jean Wagner continued. "I drew him down into that cellar over and over. I got him to jump in that damn well. Got more of assface's wolves to attack him and Lucas out on the Maumee after you sent 'em out there to *retrieve Lucas' memories*. Did better acting in these last few weeks than he ever did out in Hollywood. I gave him even more fake memories. I've lied my tail off and used every trick in my damn bag to get him to leave again. It ain't my damn fault he's made of sturdier shit than every other damn witch before him, is it? What kind of fuckin' moron—no matter how powerful—sticks around through all of that?"

"One who's in love."

"Oh, blow me." Esther Jean waved Carlita off. "That's the dumbest shit I've heard in my whole fuckin' life—and that's a long damn time. The bar is pretty fuckin' high."

Carlita chuckled. "I'll miss this."

"Yeah." Esther Jean shrugged. "Me, too. But it ain't my fault my magics wasn't strong enough for him not to see through, damnit. By mornin', he'll remember everything—even if I don't help him. And it won't be the shit we want him to think he remembers, either. Then we'll really be fucked, won't we?"

"What about Lucas?" Carlita asked, chewing at her lip thoughtfully.

"He ain't strong enough to see through shit. Not yet. Probably that damn vegetarian diet." Esther Jean sighed. "But Rob will help him."

"Lucas ain't meat starved. He's inexperienced." Carlita rolled her eyes. "And Rob will help him because he loves him."

Esther Jean threw her hands in the air.

"I didn't expect that to be real, all right?" She bellowed. Wolves cowered. "Who knew that's the magic they'd choose not to see through?"

"Sometimes, first love sticks."

"That's the dumbest shit I've ever heard."

"You may be powerful, Esther Jean," Carlita said. "But even you don't know everything. Maybe Rob and Lucas really were in love when they were kids. They weren't just going through the motions as most kids do. Your fake memories couldn't change true love."

Again, Esther Jean's hands were thrown in the air.

"No bother." Carlita waved her off. "Things will still go as they are supposed to go."

Esther Jean shook her head, a concerned look on her face.

"He may be strong, Carlita." She said. "But he ain't ready. Maybe if he'd stayed gone another ten years...but he'll do what he's supposed to do...because he's a good boy...but he ain't strong enough to stop *him*. This time, we ain't winnin'."

"Do we ever?" Carlita asked. "Really?"

"Well, no."

"Then," Carlita sighed, "this time will be no different."

"I suppose not." Esther Jean said with finality. "Our plans have gone to shit, damnit."

Carlita stepped back, as though ending their meeting, but her eyes landed on Esther Jean's once again.

"What?" Esther Jean snapped.

"It's a shame, really."

"An apocalypse is always a shame."

"No." Carlita shook her head. "You actually loved this one. He was special, wasn't he?"

Esther Jean just stared back at Carlita.

"I think you might have even believed he would end all of us." She added. "Eventually. If he had just stayed away long enough to mature more."

"Well," Esther Jean replied evenly, her eyes boring into Carlita's, "we'll never know now, will we?"

For several moments, Carlita and Esther Jean stared at each other, and a pack of confused werewolves cowered in the periphery. Finally, with an air of finality, Carlita shrugged.

"There's still time."

"Hours." Esther Jean scoffed. "We got hours."

"Rob will know sacrifice," Carlita said simply. "But maybe he won't be alone in that this time. Unlike you, I'm an oracle. I know when there's reason to hope."

Esther Jean didn't have a chance to respond. Carlita simply disappeared into the shadows, a plume of dust billowing into the air where she once stood. Esther Jean shook her head at the now empty spot that Carlita had once occupied. Sacrifice. Yes. Rob would know sacrifice. Just like every other witch before him, reaching back to the dawn of human existence. There was no way around that fact. Sighing to herself, Esther Jean turned on her heels to stride away from whence she came, the pack of wolves catching her eye.

"Well?" She snapped at them, making them all shiver. "Scat, ya' assholes! Go mark your territory or some shit! Tell your master I said to go fuck himself!"

Each wolf let out a yelp, as though having been kicked in the behind, then they all scattered, disappearing into the dark. They were not nearly as dramatic or graceful as the oracle had been. Esther Jean stood there in the now empty parking lot, the chilly early Spring breeze forcing her to wrap her arms around herself as she looked up at the orange moon. The ground had stopped shaking, but she knew that didn't mean anything had changed.

"*Why'd ya' have to take Lucas with ya', ya' damn fool?*" She said to no one. "*You would-a got out of here if you hadn't.*"

With a grumble and a "clop-clop" sound from her gardening clogs, she stomped back in the direction from which she came.

# Chapter 2

*Nelda Hammersmith wore glasses when I first arrived in Hollywood. Big spectacles that made her eyes look like they were staring out at me from behind fish bowls. Even then, as we had our first meeting, I knew that she didn't need the glasses. Mrs. Hammersmith, agent to some of the biggest and brightest stars in the universe that was Hollywood, liked to make statements. Sometimes those statements simply announced what an odd duck she was, but they were statements nonetheless. As I remember it, I don't recall how I found my way to Nelda's office in the heart of Los Angeles. I didn't remember much of my trip from Ohio to California. In fact, I couldn't even remember if I took a plane or rode in a car…I just knew that I had decided to leave Point Worth for Hollywood, and that was all there was to it.*

*Then I was in Nelda Hammersmith's office, telling her I wanted to be a star.*

*At first glance, she simply sniffed at me, appalled that some kid off of the street would be so brazen as to demand anything of an agent of her caliber. Seconds later, a cloud seemed to pass over Nelda's face…and then I was suddenly being proclaimed the Hot New Thing she had been waiting to discover.*

*You don't have anywhere to live in L.A.?*
*You can stay with me!*
*You're not old enough?*
*We'll lie!*
*Make up a backstory!*
*Change your name!*

*Suddenly, I was Nelda Hammersmith's new best friend who was going to help her become even richer—and hopefully, myself along the way. Even when she said my scene reads weren't all that great or my voice wasn't stellar, she looked hungry.*

*I had "IT."*

*That intangible, elusive thing that the biggest stars always possessed.*

*Nelda Hammersmith told me that if I "stuck with her," there wasn't anything I couldn't achieve in show business.*

*So...I stuck with her.*

*The Rolling Stones* were playing on the radio when I was suddenly jolted awake in the passenger seat of my car. Lucas had obviously hit a pothole or speedbump because I was jostled in my seat, and my eyes flew open as the seatbelt bit into my chest. As one does in such situations, after the evening—and I guess proceeding weeks—we had endured, I looked around frantically, expecting an attack of some kind. Had Jason and his wolves caught up to us in their trucks, and were they now attempting to run us off the road? They were all dumbass country boys with pickup trucks, so I didn't feel that it was beyond them to attempt to spin us out, roleplaying their favorite NASCAR fantasies. They probably even had a wad of dip in their protruded lips with Gatorade bottles full of dip spit snuggled securely between their thighs as they slammed into my much smaller car. Or worse, cups filled with spit-soaked paper towels tucked between their legs. My mind raced, wondering if we had become complacent and hadn't expected them to come after us. I had fallen asleep so suddenly as Lucas drove that it was apparent I had let my guard down. A person who had gone through the day I just had would have to be stupid to just fall asleep and expect to be safe while they slumbered.

Of course, I had never claimed to be smart.

Lucas chuckled, though it was tense and slightly higher in pitch than normal as he glanced over at my worried expression and the crazy whipping around of my head as I looked all around. In my frenzy, it took a moment for me to realize that he was simply driving us east on the dark and deserted highway 2 towards Cleveland. We had just needed to get out of Point Worth and get to Hopkins airport so that we could fly to Los Angeles. Put as many miles between us and our former lives as we could, as quickly as we could. Of course, I didn't know how long I had been asleep or what had jostled me awake, so I had no idea how close to Cleveland we were when I awoke. Cleveland is no Los Angeles, but it is big enough that if we were nearby, I would at least see the lights in the distance. But the road and horizon ahead of us were dark.

"What's wrong, babe?" Lucas managed to mumble.

"Did you hit something?" I turned to him, trying to calm myself down. "I felt a bump."

"Must've been a big bump."

More nervous chuckling.

"So...you did hit something?"

"No." He turned his head to glance at me briefly, a worried expression chasing away the brief look of amusement. "You just startled awake, Rob. I didn't hit anything. You must have been having a bad dream."

"How long was I asleep?" I frowned to myself as my fingers found their way through my hair, pushing it off of my forehead.

"Um," Lucas frowned, "I don't remember when you fell asleep. But I've been driving for, like, maybe an hour?"

Turning my head briefly to glance out of the windshield, I looked out at the road before us. My eyes darted to either side of the road, taking in nothing but darkness around us.

"We should be getting kind of close to Cleveland," I said as I turned back to Lucas. "Right?"

"Right." He gave me a firm nod as his eyes stared out at the road before us. "We'll go straight to Hopkins, babe."

"Two one-way tickets." I smiled at him, but there was an uneasiness in my gut.

"We'll be in L.A. before the sun peeks over the ocean." He smiled happily as he steered.

"Maybe." I chuckled, trying to remind myself that we were safe. "I don't know when the next direct flight to L.A. is."

"Take anything." His eyes darted over to me nervously, though he tried to keep his focus on the darkness ahead of us. "I don't care if there are layovers or stops or anything."

"You're nervous." I reached over and laid my hand on his thigh, letting my fingers give him a reassuring squeeze. "I am, too."

"I—Rob, I just want out of this state. Ever since we drove out of Point Worth, I've wanted to throw up. I know if we can put some miles between us and that town, I'll feel better."

"I know what you mean." I nodded slowly, patting his leg. "Do you want to pull over and let me drive the rest of the way? So you can relax?"

"I'm not stopping this car unless it's in a parking spot at Hopkins." He chuckled, though he seemed less nervous.

"All right."

We sat in silence, my hand laid on his thigh as Lucas drove us down highway 2, trying to put further distance between us and our hometown.

"Hey," Lucas grumbled. "Talk to me. Give me something to think about besides...*everything else.*"

"You know," I began, "we could live really close to the ocean. We could get a place in Malibu or something, where we could step right out of our backdoor and...*boom*...ocean."

"That would be nice." He sighed dreamily.

"We could sit on our deck or in our backyard, sipping wine, snuggled up, listening to the ocean. Smelling and tasting the salt in the air. Watch the sunrise and sunset every day. Maybe we will get a dog."

Lucas was smiling widely out at the road before us, though I was worried his eyes were focused on something only he could see.

"Cook dinners together and read on the sofa with our new dog draped over our laps, and—"

"Big dog, eh?"

"You want a Pomeranian?"

"I like all dogs."

"Well, you can decide which dog we will adopt." I smiled at him. "And then we'll go upstairs when it's bedtime, lock the dog out of the bedroom, and do disrespectful things to each other. Every. Single. Night."

Lucas' smile was even brighter.

"After the disrespecting, we can let the dog in, though, right?" His eyes practically twinkled at the thought. "We don't want him to have to sleep alone."

"What do you have against girl dogs?" I teased.

"Him or her. Either or."

"Yes. He or she could still sleep with us once the disrespectful behavior is over, babe."

Lucas sighed happily.

"I love our life in L.A. already."

"I do, too." I squeezed his thigh. "Are you okay now?"

"Better."

"Are you going to be okay?"

"It'll take time." He replied. "But, yeah. I just...I mean...Point Worth is my home, Rob. Grandpa will—I'm going to miss some people. That's all."

"You can always call him when we get to L.A. He can come visit us."

"What about Mrs. Wagner?"

"No." I slid my hand from his thigh.

Lucas glanced over at me, nervously.

"What happened?"

"I don't want to talk about it." I shook my head.

"Babe..."

"She's not my grandmother, Lucas," I stated a little more sharply than I had intended. "I don't know how I know that...but I know it."

"How can you know something but not know how you know it?" He asked gently, obviously not wanting to fight, but also wanting answers he had a right to hear. "I mean, that's weird, right?"

"I guess."

"Rob, you forget that we have some of the same memories. If Mrs. Wagner wasn't your grandmother, don't you think that would be scratching around in my mind, too? I have no reason to think she's not, babe. That's weird, too, right?"

"Well, yes." I agreed. "I think maybe I'll figure things out once we have some time and distance between Point Worth and us."

"Why?"

"Lucas," I was chewing at my lip, "things haven't been right in my head, memory-wise, since I came back to that fucking shithole town. I thought I knew what my previous life was like, then I realized our memories were…I don't know? Fucked up?"

"But we have our memories back."

"Yeah. I mean. Yeah. We do."

Lucas gave me a suspicious look out of the corner of his eye.

"What?" I laughed a little too sharply.

"You don't seem convinced that we have all of our memories back."

"It's not that."

"Then what?"

"Just forget it." I turned my head, looking behind us. "I mean, I'm just all foggy from…everything. Right? Once we're out of Ohio, I'll feel differently about everything."

"*You've gotta be kidding me.*"

"I just need some distance. That's all." I could see lights off in the distance behind us.

That was odd.

"*No. No. No. No.*"

"Babe," I turned around to look at Lucas, "don't get all pissy with me, all right? I'm just all wonky in my head right now. That's all."

"*Fucking shit!*" Lucas growled, which made my eyes triple in size.

Lucas slammed on the brakes of my car, forcing me to turn and brace my hands against the dashboard to keep from being sent through the windshield. The sound of squealing tires against asphalt filled the interior of the car as I held onto the dashboard, and Lucas brought the car to a full stop. When we had come to a complete stop, I was still staring at Lucas, even more wide-eyed than before, and my fingers refused to be pried from the dash. Lucas' hands were no longer on the steering wheel and were slowly curling into fists, and his face had turned red with rage.

*What the fuck was going on with him?*

"*Fuck. Fuck. Fuck. FUCK!*" Lucas punctuated each curse with a slamming of his fist against the steering wheel, ratting it on the mount.

"What the hell is going on?" I gasped, finally pulling my hands away from the dashboard. "Lucas—"

"FUCK!"

Lucas ripped the driver's side door open and leapt from the car. Before I could react, he was stomping towards the front of the car. Quickly, I turned in my seat so that I could open my door and leap out of the car to chase after him. The last thing I wanted was for Lucas to march off into the darkness in a rage—for whatever reason—and then have to spend even more time in Ohio. When I turned to get at my door, my eyes darted to look out of the windshield once again. Lucas was standing in front of the car, his fists balled up in rage as he stared off at the side of the road.

*What the fuck had caught his eye?*

That's when I saw the sign.

"YOU'RE NOW LEAVING POINT WORTH, OHIO. THE SMALLEST TOWN WITH THE BIGGEST HEART. HOPE WE MEET AGAIN."

*What the actual fuck?*

*When I was a young boy, my mother loved playing music whenever she did any chores around the house. Of course, her favorite bands and artists were from the 60s, 70s, and 80s. Sometimes she'd played some 90s rock and pop, but more often than not, bands like* The Rolling Stones, The Beatles, Fleetwood Mac, Aretha Franklin, The Supremes, The Police, The Pretenders, The Mamas and the Papas, Bruce Springsteen, *and* John Cougar Mellencamp *would be heard coming from whatever device she was listening to music on at the time. From a very young age, I couldn't remember the house not being full of music, dancing, and laughing as my mom puttered around, doing everything she could to make it a happy and fun home for my dad and me.*

*Mom would wash dishes as* Don't Sleep in the Subway *by* Petula Clark *played in the background. Her hips would shimmy, and her feet would never stop moving as her head rolled around, and her hands washed and dried dishes. If it hadn't been for the fact that I grew up in the late 90s and early aughts, this wouldn't have been that odd. The fact that my mother was born in the late 60s—thus, had not been born, or at least, had not been that old when a lot of her favorite songs had been recorded—was odd, too, I suppose. However, my mother loved the music she loved, and there was no point in questioning it. Of course, I was very young when my mother was still around, so I didn't know at the time that her taste in music was unusual for her age. I just loved the happiness and dancing. I loved that, as a child, my mother encouraged me to dance and sing and prance around the house, carefree and happy.*

*My mother encouraged my father to react with happiness and joy instead of anger and frustration when he was having a bad day. Instead of raising voices or complaining, we would eat and listen to music. Then we would dance and clean up as a family, though I was too small to really be of much help. Then I would groan as my parents shared a kiss at the sink, happy to be alive, married to their favorite person, and to have a home we all adored. My life with my parents was brief, but it was joyful.*

*It was the childhood everybody should have growing up.*

*But then my mother mostly disappeared from my memory after something…strange…rattled and shook our house.* Every Little Thing She Does Is Magic *by* The Police *had been playing when it happened.* I *don't really remember the exact moment that was the last time I saw her, but I remember being in the kitchen with her when the house began shaking...then I was being put to bed by my father.*

*The following morning, he was gone, too.*

*And a strange woman was there in his stead.*

*Why had my parents left me?*

*Where did they go?*

*Why would someone do that to such a young child?*

"Fuck, fuck, fuck, fuck, fuck, fuck," Lucas chanted angrily as he stared at the sign and I slid out of the car in disbelief.

Instinctively, I wanted to go to Lucas and comfort him, to calm him down and keep him from getting more upset than he already was presently. I wanted to tell him that maybe he had just somehow driven in a circuitous route and brought us back to Point Worth. No big deal. We could get back into my car—maybe I would drive this time—and we could head out for Cincinnati again. Looking over my shoulder as I stood alongside my car, I knew that doing any of those things would be pointless. I could see the lights of Point Worth behind us—as if we had just left.

"Babe," I asked hurriedly. "Did you ever make any turns?"

Lucas was squatting down in front of the welcome side, his head in his hands as he rocked on the heels of his feet.

"No, no, no, no."

"Shit," I mumbled.

We had never left Highway 2, which ran straight through Point Worth. We would have been on a straight shot from Point Worth to Cincinnati with barely any twists or turns. The only way we could have ended up where we were is if Lucas had taken a turn, driven south, back west, then in a northern direction before turning east back towards Cincinnati. And he would have had to drive through Point Worth again in order for us to see the sign indicating the city limit of Point Worth. We hadn't gone through Point Worth again. We weren't finding ourselves by the sign due to some mistake on his part.

*Magic.*

Not the good kind.

"Fuck, fuck, fuck, fuck." Lucas was kneeling now, his hands on his knees as he rocked and cursed. "Oh, fuck, Rob."

"Hey." I shook my head to clear my negative thoughts and overall sense of impending doom. My gut was sinking towards my ankles. "Babe."

Hustling over to Lucas before he had a complete nervous breakdown, I squatted down in front of him. His head was in his hands again as the headlights of my car partially illuminated us. I reached out and pulled Lucas towards me, and he practically fell against me, as if he had no strength left in his body. Whether or not he was freaked out by the fact that he had driven for over an hour and we never even got out of Point Worth or the fact that how screwed we were was suddenly dawning on him, I knew that I couldn't let him fall apart. I wasn't sure why my brain wasn't slowly turning to mush—I had every right to flip my lid—but I just wasn't surprised.

Somewhere in the back of my mind, I had known that we would never get out of Point Worth.

Above all things, I was mad that I had convinced myself that we could. That I had allowed myself to believe it.

"It's okay, babe." I held Lucas to me as my car idled, and Lucas shook, his arms violently grabbing ahold of me, as though he needed to be reminded what was real. "It's okay."

"How the fuck are we still in Point Worth, Rob?" He managed to choke out. "How the fuck is that possible?"

Lucas wasn't crying or falling into complete hysterics. Still, it was obvious that he wasn't holding himself together as well as he would have wanted under normal circumstances. The problem was—we hadn't found ourselves cast into a normal situation since we'd had coffee at the Sunny Side-Up Café right after I got back to Point Worth. Everything that had happened since I returned to Point Worth—to Oma's—had been a complete shit show. It was like riding a rollercoaster, my return to Point Worth. At first, things are fun and different, then the cars start to move, and you find yourself going uphill, slowly, slowly, *slowly*...you see the tip of the coaster that you will soon be cresting before the fall. And you start to dread the fall.

We had found ourselves at the top of the coaster. We were slowly inching our way into the fall. Soon...there'd be no stopping the downward journey.

"I don't know."

*I knew.*

*Lucas knew.*

"Why won't this fucking place just let us leave?" Lucas growled suddenly, making me jump, though I didn't let go of him. "I knew this place would never let me go, but fuck!"

Lucas pushed away from me gently and fell back against the asphalt, his knees rising so that he could wrap his arms around them. I fell to my knees in front of him, a great gust of breath escaping my throat as I shook my head. As I knelt there in front of Lucas, only the headlights of my car providing us with any light as the city limit sign loomed over us, what Lucas had said rang through my ears. Like a fly buzzing around my ear, his words were distracting me from any other thoughts.

"What do you mean?"

"What?" Lucas barked, though his anger wasn't directed at me.

"You said you *knew this place would never let you go*?" I frowned. "What did you mean, Lucas?"

Lucas looked up, his face no longer buried against his knees, and gave me a confused look, half of his face cast in shadow.

"You said," My brow furrowed, "that you *knew this place would never let you go*. That's what you said. What did you mean? It sounds like maybe you know something you're not sharing, Lucas."

He sighed. "No. Not really. Well, it's just—"

"—something that you knew."

Lucas stared into my eyes for a few breathless moments, then nodded.

"Why?"

"Because," He sighed, "I just know things, Rob. We've talked about this, and—"

"But you said this place would never let you go. You knew that. You've never mentioned *that* before."

Lucas was sighing again, and his legs shot out, leaving him sitting like a rag doll dropped right there in the middle of the highway.

"Because it's batshit crazy, Rob." He threw his hands up. "The fact that I know things is batshit crazy. That's bad enough, okay? But then to say something like: '*Ya' know, every time I drive over to Toledo, there's this inextricable force calling me back, as though I might be violently ill if I don't return to Point Worth?*' That's craziest of all, right? Look, I know you're special and everything, magic and all that jazz, but even you would have trouble with that. Who the hell am I going to tell something like that to? Who will understand it if I say that Point Worth—*a town*—has claws and they're buried in my fucking skin, Rob?"

"Calm down, babe." I reached out to touch the toe of his shoe gently. "I just want answers. We're sitting in front of this sign, and we passed a 'welcome' sign over an hour ago. I'm trying to understand. That's all."

"Baptizing the cat?" He grinned slightly, looking down at his lap.

"Hopefully not." I chuckled, though my heart wasn't in it.

"Rob." Lucas sighed. "When you found me at the football stadium…I knew that Jason and his pack weren't going to hurt me. I knew it. Not because I'm Mystic Meg or something, but because nothing was adding up. Why would they go to all that trouble? Especially since it was obvious that they wanted you to come get me.

They wanted me with you, and they wanted to delay you leaving. They knew if they could waste time and also make sure you had me with you—you wouldn't be able to leave either. If I'm with you, you're stuck here—because this town won't let me leave. And they were delaying everything because…"

"He's coming." I nodded. "He's probably here."

"Who is he?" Lucas seemed to be pleading with the universe to give him answers.

"I don't know." I shook my head. "I mean…I know, and I don't. It's almost as if—"

"We don't really have our memories back?"

My eyes went to Lucas and were greeted with a raised, questioning brow.

"Yes."

"I've felt that, too." Lucas nodded. "You thought you went and got our memories, but I think that you only got what someone wanted you to get."

"Who?" I squinted.

"Your grandmother."

"She's not my grandmother," I replied, though it wasn't an admonishment, merely a reminder.

"Esther Jean Wagner." Lucas shrugged. "She's pulling our strings, Rob. I've known that, too."

I looked down at the asphalt, my hand still on the tip of Lucas' shoe.

"Fuck."

"Get in the car, Rob." Lucas' words drew my eyes upward to find him shaking his head solemnly. "I'll walk back into town. If you leave now, it might not be too late. Get in the car and drive as fast as—"

"You think I'd fucking leave you here?"

"You have to. I can't leave."

"Then I can't."

"Don't be ridiculous, Rob," Lucas grumbled. "Get in the fucking car and—"

"Hey," I gripped his foot tightly, "I'm not going anywhere without you. If you can't leave, I won't."

"You know that's the craziest thing you could decide, right? If you stay here, then...well, I don't know. That's one thing I don't know. My head feels cloudy. I can't see that far."

"Maybe a decision hasn't been made?" I suggested.

"Maybe. I wish..."

I couldn't help but smile.

"Be careful with wishes, babe."

Lucas smiled back. "I just wish we had the ending to the story in our hands. Then maybe...I don't know...maybe we could change it. If we knew what was coming, I mean."

"What?"

"If you know what's supposed to happen, sometimes you can change it."

"No, I mean, you said you wish you had the story in your hands?" I started to rise to my feet.

Lucas quickly followed, pushing himself up off of the ground to stand before me. Concern but also curiosity etched valleys in his face as he considered me.

"The book," I said, simply.

"Sure." He shrugged. "The book. What does that mean?"

"Books hold stories." I shook my head, trying to clear my thoughts as I marched towards the car, Lucas at my heels. "I mean, sometimes. Just, your thought about wanting to know the ending to the story. And books hold stories. I have a book."

"I have a ton of books at home." Lucas chuckled nervously from behind me as we approached the backdoor of the car. "But they're not going to do much to save us, Rob."

"This book will." I smiled to myself as I tore the car door open. "It's a spellbook."

"A spellbook?" Lucas snorted playfully. "Like a book that witches—"

I turned to him, a half-frown decorating my face. Lucas shifted on his feet.

"Sorry." He offered. "Obviously, you would have a spellbook."

"Right." I nodded as I bent down and reached into the backseat of the car to retrieve the book I had taken from Oma's—*my family's*—home. "Well, it's my family's book. I mean, I think. It's just been around as long as I can remember, and it might be able to help us. It won't give us the ending of the story, but maybe it can get us out of this fucking town. No matter who's trying to keep us here."

I lifted the heavy leather tome from the backseat and pulled it out of the car. Turning to Lucas, I smile widely as I handed it to him. Tentatively, as though he was afraid that it might bite him, Lucas took the book from me, cradling it gently in his own hands.

"Go on." I urged him. "You're the college graduate. Find us a spell that will get us out of here."

Lucas swallowed hard, steeling his resolve, before giving me a firm nod, then he fanned the book open. I watched eagerly as Lucas looked into the book, as though it would reveal the universe's secrets to him. Hell, maybe it would. I hadn't used the book in so many years, I had no idea what the book could do for us. I couldn't even remember what all was in it. All I could remember was a beautiful hand-drawn sketch of a skeletal tree in early Spring, a single flowering bud on one of the branches, near the end. It was the best hope we had for getting out of Point Worth, though. Anything that could help us cross the city lines and stay on the other side had to be a great thing. I watched as Lucas' curious expression turned to confusion as he stared down at the pages in the book. He flipped a page. Then another. Then another.

"What is it?" I asked. "Is there something that can help us?"

Lucas's brow furrowed even deeper, then he finally looked up at me.

"Rob." He shook his head. "This is, I don't know, a children's storybook? This doesn't have any, uh, spells, or anything. I mean, it literally starts with 'Once upon a time.' And there are children's drawings. Slightly morbid ones, but still."

He turned the book so I could look down at it.

"What?" I grumbled as my eyes met the pages.

As sure as Lucas had said it, the pages were filled with what looked like any ordinary children's story. Flipping pages as Lucas held the book, more writing—in a fancy script, but stories nonetheless—and pictures of ghosts and goblins leapt out to greet my eyes. The book was worthless.

*The man and woman lay on the ground, unconscious and bleeding as the boy cowered in the corner, his hands held up defensively as the hooded figure bore down on him. For hours after leaving his room, the young boy had been at the mercy of the man in the black hooded cloak. Screamed at, threatened, forced to watch his parents squirm and plead as the menacing figure tortured them until they lay on the floor, nearly lifeless and unable to do anything to protect their son. The man in the black hooded cloak never stopped grinning as he subjected the young boy to the sights and sounds of his parents being punished for his stubbornness. Of course, the boy wasn't stubborn, he had been prepared. For his entire life, as short as it had been up until that moment, he had been warned that the man in the black hooded cloak would arrive one day.*

*And he was never to willingly accept anything the man gave him.*

*No matter how greatly he was tempted.*

*No matter what the man said.*

*No matter what the man did.*

*No power was great enough to pay the price that would be asked of him.*

*So, when the man arrived, in the boy's sixth year of life, the boy said:*

*"No."*

*For hours, the man in the black hooded cloak did all that he could, after rising from his throne of gleaming white bones, to convince the boy otherwise. Even as his parents screamed in agony and writhed on the floor, the boy kept saying:*

*"No."*

*To some, it may have seemed callous that a boy of such an age would allow his parents to endure such misery. But it had been his parents who made him promise to always say:*

*"No."*

*For they knew what it meant to say:*

*"Yes."*

*There is power in words.*

*There is power in:*

*"No."*

*Yet, as his parents lay on the floor of their home, beaten and nearly broken, barely hanging onto life, the boy still refusing the offerings of the man in the black hooded cloak, it became apparent that the boy would not be broken. Yes, he might cry and scream out with guilt and fear, but he would do exactly as he had been taught all of his life. He would say:*

*"No."*

*When the man in the black hooded cloak lifted his hand, not to strike the child physically, but to deliver another kind of punishment, the boy's grandfather intervened. He pleaded with the man to give him a moment with the boy, to talk sense into him. And, under the watchful eye of the man in the black hooded cloak, the grandfather convinced his grandson to say:*

*"Yes."*

*"No" became a "yes."*

*And the man in the black hooded cloak was appeased. He gave the boy what he had come to give him. As quickly as he arrived, so he departed. And the grandfather told his grandson that he now had a new task. He was never to use his gift. To do so would make him succumb to the will of the man in the black hooded cloak. So, no matter what, he was to bury his knowledge of his gift far into his subconscious. Forget that it was there. Never speak of it. Never even think of it. And he could still yet be saved from generations of bondage and imprisonment.*

*The young boy nodded, tears rolling down his cheeks.*

*In the morning, his parents would be worse for the wear, but they would be alive. And the boy had already begun building the walls in his mind that would trap his secret. He would speak of it to no one. One day, he would forget that he ever knew his secret.*

*The man in the black hooded cloak had been fooled.*

*He had achieved what he had come to do, but the boy had proved his will was stronger than even the man in the black hooded cloak knew.*

*Even if the day came that the gift was remembered, and he spoke of it to anyone, he knew what he would do.*

*And that would be anything but serve the man in the black hooded cloak.*

*Power unused has only one thing to do.*

*Grow.*

*What once was a seed delivered to the soil by a passing bird becomes a mighty Sequoia that shades the woodland creatures.*

*What once belonged to no one ends up belonging to everyone.*

*What once had a particular purpose ends up deciding its own fate.*

*There is power in stubbornness.*

*There is power in:*

*"No."*

Lucas said nothing when I violently threw the book into the backseat floorboard of the car. He said nothing as I fell into the driver's seat of my car. Even as he climbed into the passenger seat, stoic and resigned, he said nothing. We sat at the Point Worth city limits for longer than necessary, since we knew there was only one way to go—nothing else to consider. When I sighed to myself, my hand reaching for the gearshift, Lucas' hand found mine. Together, we pulled the gearshift down to reverse. Lucas' eyes met mine:

"I love you." He said.

"I love you, too," I replied. "More than anything else."

A quick kiss, a lingering glance, and I slowly backed up, turned the car around, and pointed us towards Point Worth once more.

If we couldn't leave as one, we would stay together.

Maybe that upset Lucas, feeling as though he had conscripted me when my fate had been decided, but it wasn't his fault. I could have left if I wanted to go. But, without Lucas, my life in Hollywood would have slowly turned into the living nightmare it had been before. I would rather stay in Point Worth. Face whatever was to come. I knew what waited in Hollywood. At least in Point Worth, I knew there was a chance for something better. Even if we had to walk through Hell to get to it.

At least my hand would be holding his in this version of Hell.

# Chapter 3

"Well," Carlita crossed her arms over her chest, "ain't that some shit?"

She stared down at the long crevice running along the middle of Main Street, steam rising in ribbons from the depths below. No wider than a man's foot, the crevice was still a concern, especially since there was no way to tell its depth. Of course, anytime such a crack appears in a road oft-traveled, people have reason to be concerned. The ground shifts, too much rain or too little rain, man-made disasters like fracking and drilling, anything can cause a road to develop the beginnings of a canyon. These types of things usually happen in states with frequent or powerful earthquakes, not in small towns in Ohio, though. There was no logical reason for the crack to be threading its way down Main Street, but logic had no home in Point Worth.

"It's some shit." Jackson Barkley gave a firm nod as he stood at Carlita's right. "It's a whole pile of evil horseshit."

"Mmm." Carlita agreed, her eyes not wandering from the steaming crack.

"I don't like this." Andrew piped up from her left. "I mean...this is fucked up, right? Even with all things considered, this is some end of days shit, right?"

Carlita slowly turned her head, her eyebrow rising as her eyes met his.

"Sorry." Andrew shrugged, then shivered.

"He's coming," Carlita said simply in Andrew's direction before turning to look at the gaping crack once again. "We all knew it was an inevitability."

"You've had a little longer to adjust to it than I have," Andrew muttered.

Jackson Barkley gave a dry chuckle.

"Well," Carlita fluttered a hand in the air like a butterfly's wings, "things still have a way of feeling like they creep up on you, baby."

"What do we do now, Carlita?" Jackson asked. "We could warn people, couldn't we?"

"They all know this is coming." She said.

"But," Mr. Barkley harrumphed, "it still ain't right to not warn them."

"They made their bed," Carlita answered sharply. "Let 'em lie in 'em."

"I suppose." Jackson sighed.

"We all know whose fault this is," Andrew grumbled. "The-fucking-Council. And Jason. His pack. Goddamn Esther Jean Wagner."

Carlita grinned.

"Goddamn Esther Jean Wagner." She repeated. "You forget Rob and Lucas."

"It's not their fault." Andrew shoved his hands into his pockets.

He had been shaking since he had met Carlita and Jackson on Main Street and had to do something to hide that fact.

"The bird learned a new song to sing." Jackson nudged Carlita impishly.

She chuckled.

"Shut up." Andrew rolled his eyes.

In unison, all of their eyes went back to the crack that ran down the middle of the street. The ground rumbled, and the crack spread wider.

"It's too late for warning or blame, kids." Carlita tossed her hands up in the air. "And we promised vieja loca that we would do what we could. So…let's do what we can."

"We're all gonna die." Andrew snorted.

"Maybe not." She said.

"Well," Jackson shrugged, "I'm older than most. Present company excluded."

Carlita patted his arm gently, smiling warmly at the old man.

"Ya' know," Jackson said, "I should really be mad at you and Esther Jean right now, Carlita—"

"Yeah?"

"—but I just can't bring myself to be mad. Y'all did your best, I suppose."

Carlita gave him a warm smile.

"Well, we'll see what the dawn brings before we claim it to be our best, shall we?"

He nodded, a smile coming to his lips.

The ground shook again, making all three of them step back as the crack in the street widened a few more inches.

"It's been nice knowing you fellas," Carlita said. "Just in case I don't get to tell you both later."

"Back atcha." Jackson croaked.

Andrew merely groaned.

*The man in the black hooded cloak knew how to get his way. Promises and threats, torture if those methods did not produce results. Killing those who opposed him was a last resort, but one he gleefully indulged in whenever the mood struck. When the pack—only seven when they arrived—showed up in Point Worth, the man in the black hooded cloak saw his opportunity.*

*Add to his growing army.*

*Though he was unable to negotiate for himself, The Council met with the pack alpha. Offered them their greatest desires. The only price was allegiance to Bloody Bones.*

*The alpha responded swiftly. Courageously. For his pack was few in numbers compared to The Council.*

*Allegiance would be given to no one but his own.*

*No matter the offer.*

*His pack answered to themselves and the greater good.*

*The Council's answer was just as swift. At the behest of the man in the black hooded cloak, The Council, much greater in number than the new pack, quickly slaughtered six of the new wolves. The youngest, barely a teen, fled, a few cuts and bruises the only memory of the pack to which he once belonged.*

*Laughing and braying, the Council screamed at Andrew as he ran, announcing their plans to find those that would serve...him. If he wouldn't serve, he had no place with them. He was too young for The Council to expend any worry. If other packs wouldn't join...they'd make their own.*

*Andrew ran as fast and as far as he could.*

*He would never join The Council.*

*Or the man in the black hooded cloak.*

*But, if the time should come, that someone stood against either, he would answer the call to service.*

*Even if it meant his own death.*

*He vowed vengeance.*

*All he had to do was wait for a sign of hope.*

*And, when hope arrived, it arrived as a little old lady and a drag queen who were most definitely more than they seemed.*

*They offered nothing for Andrew's allegiance except hope. But hope is the greatest payment one can receive. So, Andrew pledged his allegiance. All he had to do for his payment, was lie.*

"I'm sorry that I hurt Rob," Andrew stated blandly as he stood beside Carlita and Jackson on Main Street. "It is the only thing I regret."

"I know, baby," Carlita said. "But we've all done what we could. What we had to do. To end all of..."

She waved her hand at the crack, even wider than before, almost as wide as a man's foot is long.

"...this." Carlita finished. "Rob would forgive you if he understood."

"He would." Mr. Barkley gave a firm nod.

"I wish I'd been scarier." Andrew sighed. "Maybe he would have left the next day. Maybe I should have told him it wasn't primal instincts. I could have said that I would do it again if he was ever around when I was a wolf the next time."

"Could-a, should-a, would-a." Jackson chirped.

"He's a thick-headed one." Carlita grinned over at Andrew, though her smile was tight, fearful. "You did an excellent job, baby."

"Thank you," Andrew said softly.

"Him leaving would've just bought us more time." Carlita reached down and took Andrew's hand in hers. "That's all. Don't lose hope."

Andrew smiled down at his hand as Carlita's fingers laced through his.

"I never have." He said firmly.

"Good." Carlita sighed. "It's all we got."

The three of them stood and watched as the crack grew wider by another inch, and the ground rumbled once more. Carlita's other hand went to Jackson's, and she laced her fingers through his. Together, they all stood and watched. Waited. There was nothing they could really do but wait. They'd all played their parts—some with bigger roles than others—but now there was nothing left for them to do until he arrived. And there was only one way that would play out. Carlita knew what was to come, but she didn't dare tell her friends. Why scare them any more than was necessary?

Lucas sat rigidly upright in the passenger seat as I drove through the dark, the headlights off. We didn't want to draw any attention to ourselves unless it was necessary. Of course, it could be argued that driving down a country road in the middle of the night with your lights off will garner attention. However, in the little country town of Point Worth, Ohio, in bum-fuck-nowhere, there would be no one watching for cars with no headlights on driving down old country roads. From the city limits of Point Worth, I had driven twenty-miles-and-hour lower than the speed limit, not wanting to drive too fast so that I could react quickly if anything happened. I didn't know what we'd find as we entered back into Point Worth, but I wanted to be alert for it if something actually happened.

My mind raced with thoughts about what was going on in my hometown and what was going on with my life. When I had left Point Worth, I thought Oma was my...well, Oma. I thought I was rushing away to become a movie star because I was a wild teen who did what he wanted. I was chasing fame and glory and riches. As the years rolled by, it was apparent that the Hollywood lifestyle—being an international superstar—was not what I wanted. It did nothing to suit me or make me happy. Little by little, my life became a walking Hell where I didn't know what was real and what was fake. Fame can do that to a person. Having your memories fucked with makes it worse.

Memories.

What exactly from my past was real, and what was fake?

Why did my memories keep changing and shifting?

Why couldn't I stick a pin in them, tack them down so that I could tell what was really going on in my life? What had gone on in my past?

As I drove us further, I decided that I was going to assume everything I knew about myself and my past was a lie.

Then again, what good would that do? The only thing I could be certain of was that I had no way of knowing if the memories I had were true or not. Everything I thought I knew was up for debate, as far as I was concerned. Was anything I remembered from my childhood true—or was it all the things I was supposed to believe? Of course, I knew one thing for certain—Lucas wasn't wrong in saying that Oma had everything to do with our fucked-up memories. I didn't know how and I didn't know why—but she had done...*something*...to our memories. But, obviously, she had fucked with the memory of what it was she had done to our memories, too. If we had ever known what that was in the first place.

Because of that, there was no reason to not believe that everything I thought I knew was false. When Lucas slid his hand across the car and laced his fingers through mine, I realized something else. Not everything was a lie. Not every memory was false. I didn't have whatever gift my boyfriend had, but some things I knew for certain, too, because something deep inside me told me that they were true. Lucas and I did love each other. There was nothing inside of me that doubted that fact. Of course, I had no idea if our memories of falling in love were true, but we stilled loved each other. That was all that mattered. If we had really fallen in love as kids, that was fine. If we had only fallen in love once I moved to Point Worth and we had false memories about everything else, that was fine.

I loved Lucas.

Period.

And I knew he loved me.

Like Lucas, some things I just knew.

"Babe," Lucas exhaled heavily, "what are we going to do?"

"I don't know," I admitted, my fingers clenching his tightly for a moment. "But we'll figure it out, right?"

"Right."

"We can't go to Oma's." I shook my head. "That would...that's just a bad idea. I mean...I don't know what she's up to or why she's up to whatever she's doing, but without the Kobolds there—"

"Ernst and the other creatures?"

"Right." I nodded, one hand steering and the other clenching Lucas' hand. "Without them, it's a dangerous place."

"Yeah," Lucas whispered. "I don't really get what you mean by that."

I sighed.

"I don't know if this is true or not. Okay?" I glanced at Lucas. He nodded sharply. He understood. "But...the Kobolds were tied to, uh, magic that was, uh, tied to the land there. They're gone now. The magic is disappearing. If they're gone, and the magic is disappearing—or gone now—something bad is going to happen. I just don't know what."

"That's..."

"Batshit crazy?" I laughed nervously.

"Well, yes." Lucas chuckled with me. "But it's also not much to make a plan on, Rob. If we don't know what's going to happen, how do we decide what we should be doing?"

"We know that...*he*...is coming."

Lucas breathed out heavily, a moaning, hissing sound.

"What?"

"You said before that I met him, or might have met him, or that the Barkley's have something to do with him," Lucas mumbled. "I just don't remember. I mean...not everything."

"What do you remember?"

"Anytime you mention him, I can visualize him in his cloak. The hood. Red, glowing, piercing eyes. But I don't know why or what memory that comes from." Lucas shivered. "That has to mean that I have seen him before. Met him. Right? Otherwise, how would I be able to visualize him?"

"I don't know. Is that something maybe you just know so you can see him?"

"No."

"Then I assume that the Barkleys are just as involved as the Wagners, right?" I nodded. "You must have met him. I think you met him when you were a child. I had a dream...or vision...or something, Lucas. When you were a child."

I glanced over to find Lucas chewing frantically at his lip.

"We're close to it." Lucas looked up. "Let's just go to my house. Right there."

Lucas's hand slipped from mine so that he could point at the road up ahead. Sure enough, the turn to Lucas' house was coming up. Giving Lucas a nod, I eased my car into the turn and headed towards Lake Erie.

"Will we be safe there?" I asked nervously as the dirt road caused the car to bounce and shimmy. "I mean…a whole window is missing."

Lucas snorted.

"I just want to get my phone." He said. "We don't have to stay if you don't want to, babe."

"It's as safe as anywhere else, I guess." I shrugged. "But why do you need your phone?"

"Maybe I can call mom or dad." He explained. "Maybe they will—"

"Maybe they will what?" I turned my head to look at him, urging him on with my eyes.

"Shit." Lucas winced. "Rob. Look."

"What?" I turned my head to look out of the windshield.

Red and yellow light was what I saw before I realized I was looking at flames shooting into the sky ahead. Something big was on fire. And there was only one thing at the end of the dirt road that was big enough to create a fire massive enough to be seen that far away. Lucas' house was on fire. Surprisingly, Lucas didn't punch the dashboard or bang his head against his window. He didn't show any signs that what we were about to drive up on had affected him in any way. As we drew closer to his property, and we pushed past the line of trees, we could finally see the base of the fire. Lucas' beautiful home on the lake was an inferno.

"Oh, shit, Lucas." I moaned as I slowed the car to a stop, at least thirty yards from his house. "Oh, fuck. I'm so sorry. What—"

"Jason." Lucas' eyes were like daggers as he stared out of the windshield towards his burning home. "His fucking pack did this."

Fire danced and flickered in Lucas' eyes.

I wanted to tell Lucas that maybe he was overreacting or just making assumptions based on anger. Instead, I nodded firmly. He was right. We both knew that Jason's pack had done this. A knot in my stomach made me wonder if Oma's house wasn't also one big bonfire. For the briefest of moments, I felt guilty for being so angry with the woman who claimed to be my grandmother. Hopefully, she hadn't been in the house if it had been set ablaze. Something told me that if Jason or his pack snuck onto the property, though, the house wasn't what got set on fire. A devilish smile curled up the corner of my mouth as I stared out at the flames licking off of the roof of Lucas' home.

"Shit, Rob!" Lucas gasped. "Look."

"What?"

Lucas was pointing out at the scene before us, his finger nearly touching the windshield.

"They're still here!" Lucas announced in a panic.

Finally, my eyes landed on what Lucas had seen. Four men—conspicuously wearing only pants—were dancing jubilantly around the fire they had obviously started. The two of us watched as the four men danced around the house, howling up at the flames that licked towards the sky, proud of the destruction they had caused. They were far enough off that I had to focus my eyes, but I finally was able to see that Jason was not with them. It was just four members of his pack.

"Get us out of here, Rob." Lucas hissed. "Let's go."

"Okay." I nodded furiously. "Okay."

"Go, go, go!" Lucas urged me on. "If they see us—"

As I moved to put the car in reverse, so that I could creep away from the fiery scene on Lucas' property, two things happened. My hands slipped, and I simultaneously hit the horn, a brief, barking blast emanating from under the hood, and I accidentally flipped on the headlights.

"Jesus Christ, Rob." Lucas groaned.

"Sorry! Sorry!" I gasped, reached for the gearshift.

Once I had the car in reverse and had eased off the brake, about to give the car gas, my eyes shot up to look out of the windshield once more. All four of the pack members had spotted us—obviously—and were running at full speed towards the car.

"Oh, fuck." Lucas groaned. "Floor it, Rob!"

My foot hit the gas, and the car shot backward. There wasn't time to react in any other way, to devise any other plan. As I slammed on the gas and the car lurched backward like a slingshot, I felt, more than saw, the first of the wolves jump on the hood of the car. The passenger side window shattered inwards, and Lucas bellowed loudly.

# Chapter 4

*Screams reached Jason's ears as he stumbled out of the circus tent, clutching his bleeding arm, breathing raggedly, his eyes out of focus as he did his best to stay on his feet. CARNAVAL was in full swing, the rides—sans riders—swooped and swirled, their lights shooting a dazzling array of lights into the night sky. The screams of the two boys were getting further away. Freshly popped popcorn, fresh cotton candy, funnel cakes, corn dogs, and other carnival treats perfumed the air as Jason fells to his knees, his vision like that of a person underwater.*

*Why did he hurt so bad?*

*He'd just been bitten once.*

*Before he got away.*

*Jason gasped and clutched his chest as a sharp pain shot through his body like a lightning bolt. He bowed his head, trying to focus on the ground, doing anything he could to clear his vision.*

*What had happened? He suddenly couldn't remember.*

*Shaking his head and trying to clear his thoughts, he did his best to let his mind ride the waves of pain shooting through his chest.*

*Something was wrong.*

*He'd been bitten.*

*By a...wolf?*

*Where'd the wolf come from?*

*He'd been watching the circus performers. Why had there been a wolf in the freaking circus?*

*The posters.*

*On Main Street.*

*They'd been everywhere.*

*The carnival—CARNAVAL—had come to town. They had set up fences and rides and stands and tents out on the old Owens' land by the lake. The posters had invited all high school-age children to come participate in the carnival for free. Jason had gotten a few of his friends together, and they all decided to go check it out. They were the only students to show up...except for that Lucas kid who was just starting out in football. And that other kid...what was his name? Robbie. That was his name. He had shown up last. They were watching the acrobats and clowns...and...the ringmaster.*

*Something had happened. There were wolves suddenly. They had attacked everyone.*

*Jason coughed violently, holding his chest with both hands, doing his best to not topple headfirst onto the trampled down grass before him.*

*When his coughing fit past, he leaned back on his knees, looking up at the sky, watery stars and moon blurry in his vision. The screaming of the two boys—Lucas and Robbie—had suddenly gone. Had a wolf gotten them? Jason panted heavily as another wave of pain, and also nausea, coursed through his body. He looked toward the gates that led out of CARNAVAL. Maybe he could get up...get help. Get away from the wolves. Fear shot through his body, realizing that any of the wolves might stray from the tent and the easier prey...and come after him again.*

*As he looked toward the gates, even with his blurry, watery vision, he could see the figure coming towards him. He could just make out the red coat and black top hat. It was the ringmaster. Jason panted harder, clutched his chest tighter, as the man approached him at a leisurely stroll. When the ringmaster finally stopped before him, nearly close enough to reach out and touch, yet not quite, Jason looked up at him, his vision suddenly clear.*

*"Well," the ringmaster—Richart maybe?—said, "they were faster than they appeared, I'm afraid. Just disappeared. Strong magics, I assume."*

*The ringmaster laughed bitterly.*

*"Fucking Oracles and Guardians." He 'tsked.' "They always ruin a good time, you know?"*

*"What?" Jason gasped, his fingers clutching at his chest.*

*Richart bowed ever so slightly, his eyes boring into Jason's.*

*"No matter." Richart sniffed the air. "You'll do. I'm going to give you a choice, Jason Morris. You must make the right decision. And you must do it quickly."*

*Jason shivered at the sound of something with more than two legs sauntering out of the tent.*

*"I need your allegiance." Richart smiled wickedly.*

Lucas yanked the sleeve of his shirt from the wolf's teeth as I spun the car around. I wanted to help him, but I couldn't drive the car and also fight the wolf who was trying to yank him out of the car. For once, I was going to have to trust that Lucas could handle himself. Besides, when I looked up, throwing the car into "Drive," my eyes locked on the red, glowing eyes of a wolf clinging to the hood of the car. *How the fuck was it holding on without human hands?* The screech of metal let me know that a werewolf's claws were good for finding purchase on almost anything. My lip turned up in a snarl as I hit the gas again, flinging us forward like a cannonball.

"Fuck you!" Lucas bellowed.

I saw him fling an elbow towards his window. A crunching sound let me know he had connected with the jaw of the wolf. The sound of a large animal rolling across the dirt road made me smile as we were propelled forward. The wolf clawing the hood and glaring through the windshield at me was a little tougher than the one who had tried to pull Lucas out through the window.

"Hold on!" I screamed before slamming on the brakes.

My car shuddered violently along the dirt road, skidding to a stop. The suddenness of our deceleration took the wolf by surprise, and it rolled from the hood of the car to land in a heap in the road before us.

"Seatbelt!" I screamed as I reached for mine and latched it quickly.

The second I heard Lucas' seatbelt click into place, I heard and felt something leap onto the back of the car. The wolf in the road before us was drunkenly stumbling to its...*paws?* Gunning the car again, I gripped the steering wheel until my knuckles were white, my teeth clenching as I aimed directly at the wolf before us. Lucas screamed out—either in fear or victory, I wasn't sure—as the front of my car plowed into the werewolf. A loud crunch and a strangled yelp reached my ears as blood splattered the windshield. I didn't take my foot off of the gas. As if going over the world's boniest, fleshiest speedbump, we were launched a few feet upwards before the car crashed down on the road once more.

"Flat meat," I stated simply as I kept my foot on the gas, urging the car away from Lucas' property.

"Rob!" Lucas gasped as he turned his head to look behind us. "There's one holding onto the trunk!"

"Why wouldn't there be?" I grumbled. "Hold on!"

Again, I slammed on the brakes. The wolf holding onto the back of the car with its claws smashed into the back window, splintering the glass, nearly sending it through and into the backseat. But its claws were pulled from the hood of the car as the stop jerked its body forward. Lucas yelped as I hit the gas again, sending the wolf rolling away. I was breathing heavily, my heart beating in my throat as I pushed my foot to the floor atop the gas pedal. Lucas had smashed one in the jaw. I had run one over. We had just seen another fly off of the back of the car, totally dazed and bloody.

Just as I expected, the fourth wolf made its presence known.

My window shattered as the wolf ran up alongside the car and threw its body against the moving vehicle. Lucas and I both screamed out in terror as glass shards rained inwards, and the car lurched up onto two wheels for a brief second.

*Goddamnit, these guys are big.*

*And fast.*

I had to keep my hands on the steering wheel to have any chance of keeping us on the bumpy dirt road, and the werewolf was running up alongside the car once more. Any second, I knew it was going to shove its jaws through the shattered window and bite me. Game over. I had no idea if I was immune to werewolf bites like Lucas—but we didn't have the time or desire to find out. Just as the werewolf came up alongside the car, panting and huffing, running at top speed—way too fast for any animal—it turned its head. I saw a flash of glowing red eyes as it lunged. Lucas' hand was suddenly on my forearm, and he was leaning across me, toward the window, one of his hands outstretched. He screamed out animalistically as magic coursed through my arm and into him, and fire erupted from his hand, a column of heat plowing into the werewolf, setting it ablaze and sending it tumbling away into the darkness.

My eyes shot over to Lucas as I thought of a burning pile of werewolf tumbling into the woods.

*Fuck it.* I thought. *Let the entire town burn down. I'm not turning into a werewolf today. If I can...*

"Go, Rob!" Lucas yelped as he positioned himself back in his seat. "Just go!"

"All right." I swallowed hard, keeping my foot pressed to the floor as I turned sharply off of the road to Lucas' house and onto the main road.

Pulling onto the main road that led out to Lucas' lands, I didn't let up off of the gas. Screaming down the road in the middle of the night in my busted-up car would surely attract the attention of any cop that might be out and about, looking for drunk drivers or someone else to ticket, but I didn't care. I wasn't going to stop until I was certain we were far enough away from the wolves. There was no point in keeping ourselves near an unsafe situation for fear that the cops might pull me over. With the mood I was in, and considering the adrenaline pumping through my veins, I would likely fight any cop that tried to stop us. Especially Sheriff Dennard.

"Damnit, Rob." Lucas bellowed to be heard over the wind whistling through the broken windows. "I'm bleeding."

Shooting a glance at Lucas, I mostly kept my eyes on the road ahead of us as I navigated the mostly straight, yet narrow two-lane road. There was no point in getting away from the wolves only to crash my car and have us out in the open like sitting ducks with no working vehicle.

"What?" I screamed back. "Did you cut yourself?"

"I guess one of 'em bit me." He returned. "Probably the one that I bashed in the face with my elbow."

He tried to twist his body so that he could show me that his right elbow was soaked in blood. I grimaced as I looked at his elbow, then realized his face was ashy-white. Nodding at him, I knew that we had to tend to his wound before we did anything else.

"Let me find a safe place, and we'll pull off, okay?"

"Okay."

For a few more miles, I skirted the northern perimeter of the Point Worth city limits, looking for somewhere secluded and hidden so that I could pull off of the road. A place where no one who might happen by and see the car easily.

Finally, as I drove along, I noticed a break in the tree line. An old service road to one of the many unused boat docks that dotted the shore of Lake Erie. I eased the speed of the car and slowly turned onto the road, killing the headlights. Slowly, I eased off of the gas as we drifted down the road, disappearing amongst the trees that lined the old road. Finally, when we were far enough within the trees, and far enough away from the road, to where I felt that we were safe, I brought the car to a full stop and put it into park. It took quite a bit of willpower to force myself to turn the car off, but I finally flicked the key. Suddenly, we were greeted by silence and darkness.

Both of us took a moment to stare out into the inky darkness before us, our breaths ragged and sharp, filling the interior of the car with the sounds of sheer adrenaline. Briefly, I wondered if the wolves wouldn't happen by, hear the sounds of the thundering hearts in our chests and the sounds of our breaths floating from the broken windows of my car, and search us out. Of course, I knew that to be ridiculous. One, the wolves were not likely to regroup and follow us so quickly after Lucas set one of them ablaze, and I had run one over. Two, they would most likely be running, and they would never hear our breathing as they ran along the road. Though our breathing sounded thunderous to my ears in the confines of the car, outside of the car, it would be hard for anyone to hear. Paranormal or not.

"Okay." I unsnapped my seatbelt and turned gently in my seat, trying to get my breathing and heartbeat under control. "Let's see your boo-boo."

Lucas smiled pitifully as he unsnapped his seatbelt and turned towards me.

"Sorry, babe." He grumbled. "I know this isn't the best time, and—"

"If he had pulled you out of the car, I don't think he was going to tie you to a football field goal post, Lucas." I shook my head. "There's nothing to be sorry for, babe. You were defending yourself. And me. It's not your fault he got you. And, even if it was your fault, fuck it. The rules don't apply when you're fighting for your life. You're allowed to be clumsy."

"I know. I know." He shook his head as he fought to not smile as he stripped his button-down off. "That was intense."

Watching Lucas undress always had an effect on me. One that was not appreciated when we had just been fighting for our lives. So, I swallowed down those feelings and simply waited as he stripped off his shirt and turned his body so that he could present his elbow. Nearly in total darkness, there was still enough light for me to see the small gash on Lucas' elbow and the darker area that was seeping blood. I couldn't help but wince at the sight as I held his arm in mine, cradling his elbow.

"Well, okay." I shrugged, still holding his arm gently. "Do it."

"Do what?"

"The thing where you borrow some of my magic and heal yourself."

"Why don't we just find something to bandage it with?" Lucas suggested. "I'm not going to bleed out, babe."

"Why not heal it while we have a moment, ya' know?"

"I don't want to use your magic." Lucas shook his head.

"You just did." I chuckled. "To set furball ablaze?"

"That was life or death." He said. "This isn't."

"Why are you giving me crap here?" I teased him. "Just do your little trick, and we won't have to worry about this any—"

"Don't you feel that, Rob?" Lucas cut me off, his voice a whisper. "Haven't you been paying attention at all tonight?"

"To what?" I asked, still examining his wound in the dark.

Lucas looked around, as though expecting someone to jump out of the velvety black woods that surrounded the car and pounce on us.

"Can't you feel it all around?" He asked again, his voice even lower. "Something is changing. Shifting. Point Worth doesn't feel the same since we first tried to drive out of here last night. It feels...emptier or something."

"Emptier?"

"Like that thing that made Point Worth...*Point Worth*...is slowly draining away. I feel like..."

I waited for the space of several breaths until a shiver danced along the back of my neck, and I couldn't take the silence any longer.

"You feel like what?"

"Like something is draining all of the magic from Point Worth." He swallowed hard.

The words felt like a knife in my gut. I wasn't sure why, but those words meant something to me.

"Don't be ridiculous." I hid a shiver by letting go of Lucas' arm and snatching up his shirt.

Lucas watched me as I ripped one of the arms off of his shirt and began wrapping it around his elbow.

"You know it's not ridiculous," Lucas stated calmly. "I can tell. I saw it in your eyes just now. Something is majorly wrong. Things are changing."

For a few moments, I focused on tying the sleeve of Lucas' shirt around his wound, making sure it was secure. A makeshift bandage, but a bandage nonetheless. Finally, I let go of his arm and looked up at him once again. Lucas' eyes were placid, he wasn't fearful. But I could tell that all of his synapses were firing. He was thinking his problem out over and over, trying to figure out why he felt the way that he felt.

"Why are you immune to werewolf bites?" I asked suddenly. "Am I?"

"Well, I don't know if you are," Lucas answered automatically.

"Don't you just know things, damnit?" I barked, which hadn't been my intention at all.

Lucas just stared back at me.

"Sorry." I corrected myself.

"I don't know, Rob," Lucas stated evenly, controlling himself. "I feel that I should, but I don't. Okay? It's like a secret locked in a cage in my mind. I feel like...I don't know...maybe I don't know on purpose."

"What does that mean?"

"Like I intentionally forgot why I'm immune."

"Why would you do that?" I snapped, again without meaning to.

"That's something else I don't know." He bit the words off sharply. "If I forgot on purpose, I probably forgot why I forgot on purpose, too, right?"

I sighed.

"But...and you won't believe me...but I'm suddenly remembering something. Jason bit me in high school. After a football game one night. I had forgotten that, too. Until now."

"Why?" I barked, not caring if anyone heard. "Why did you forget that?"

"Why did you forget you could shoot lasers and fire from your hand, Rob?" Lucas was so calm I knew that he was controlling himself for my sake, so he wouldn't snap back at me and make our situation worse. We didn't need to fight. Not now. "You don't know either. So, kindly stop giving me the third degree. I already have a bite. I don't need a burn."

He smiled impishly.

I did my best not to do it, but a smile slowly formed on my face.

"Fine." I huffed, but my heart wasn't in it. "What happened when he bit you?"

"Same thing as now." He shrugged. "Didn't you wonder why Jason was so nonchalant that night out on the Maumee when I got bit? He was too blasé about the whole thing. He knew I wasn't going to turn, even though he said it would take a few moon cycles. I told grandpa about it happening—when Jason turned into a werewolf and bit me after the game way back when. He told me to pretend it never happened. So...I just did. I forgot about it. Something...I don't know what...made it easier to do."

My brow was practically a canyon as I frowned at my boyfriend.

"Okay." I held my hands up. "But wait. I found out that those guys at the Maumee were actually Jason's. Why would he send them to bite you if he knew it wouldn't turn you into one of his pack, huh? Why go to all that trouble and risk losing two of your pack members if it wouldn't get results, Lucas? Answer that."

"It was a scare tactic."

"What was he scaring you for?"

"He was trying to scare you." Lucas shrugged.

"What?"

"Haven't you wondered why things have gotten weirder and weirder the longer you've been here, Rob?" Lucas urged me on, his eyes pleading with me. "I really think...shit. I really think everything and everyone is trying to make you leave again. But you waited too long. And you decided to take me with you. We fucked up their plans, babe."

I couldn't help it. I rolled my eyes.

"That doesn't make any sense."

"Doesn't it?" Lucas snorted. "Weird shit at Esther Jean's house. The weird cloaked person in the back yard—that we know wasn't *him*? The guy on the cliff overlooking the lake? Weird sights and sounds. Sudden werewolf attacks. Andrew? Nothing odd happened while you were gone. And Point Worth is pretty fucking odd. Then you show back up...and it's like this town is putting on a show for you, Rob. Like everyone and everything is trying to remind you why you shouldn't be here. Once we got involved...well, I got pulled into this shitstorm."

"Sorry?"

"I don't mean this is your fault, babe." His expression softened. "I just mean that I'm collateral damage."

"Fine." I threw my hands up. "Why would Oma have been so upset about me leaving? Huh? She's done nothing but give me shit nonstop for a decade for leaving Point Worth. Explain that."

"Why would she be nice to you?" He shrugged. "That would make you want to stay more. And maybe she wanted you gone, but she also hated to see you go. Having to do something and liking what you have to do are two separate things. Besides...who has been messing with our memories, babe? Santa Claus?"

"I wouldn't be the least bit surprised if he landed on the hood of this car right this second," I mumbled. "With every single goddamn reindeer in tow."

Against our will, both Lucas and I turned our eyes to look out the windshield. Suddenly, we were looking at each other and having to slap our hands over our mouths to keep from laughing at the absurdity of such a thing. Santa Claus wasn't going to appear on the hood of the car. However, with all things considered, it wasn't completely crazy to imagine it.

"Look, Rob." Lucas shook his head. "I vaguely remember the man in the black hooded cloak. But I know I'm not supposed to remember. And for a good reason, I think. Something that happened when I met him...I'm not supposed to think about. Talk about. Or remember. For my own safety. Maybe other people's safety. I don't know. But I also don't know if I made myself forget or if this is Esther Jean Wagner's work at play. I...just...don't...know."

Slowly, I breathed out, unable to connect the dots as to what was going on in the little town of Point Worth, Ohio. Or what my life was even about. Just as I had been thinking before the wolves had attacked us, Lucas put into words what I knew to be true. We couldn't trust any of our memories.

"Jason said something to me." I sighed. "Last night. When I decapitated him."

"You're going to have to get better at that." Lucas teased.

"Next time, I'm taking his head with me." I snorted. "Or burning him until he's nothing but ashes. But...he said that my magic is the only magic in town that doesn't have anything to do with...him."

Lucas was nodding along, looking thoughtful.

"Do you think," I chewed at my lip, "do you think everything in this town that is some part magical has something to do with him?"

"Maybe?"

"He's coming," I said. "Maybe he's draining all of the magic he's put out there so he can use it?"

"For what, though?"

"Well, it ain't to pull a bunny out of a hat, babe."

Lucas chuckled ruefully.

"He's planning something big," I said. "I feel like he's been stocking away ammunition...waiting for the right time...and now, he's ready to use it."

"But for what?" Lucas repeated. "If we knew what he had planned, maybe we could figure out what the hell is going on. Make some sense out of all of this. Maybe we could actually freakin' remember things, and our memories wouldn't be a fog."

Lucas and I both slumped back in our respective seats. For several minutes, we sat there, just staring out of the windshield into the darkness. Lucas finally pulled his shirt on and buttoned it, looking slightly silly with one sleeve missing. However, the choice between looking silly and bleeding was an easy choice to make.

"We have to see Esther Jean," Lucas said with finality.

"No," I said. "I can't trust her."

Lucas slumped back in his seat, a harrumph escaping his lips.

# Chapter 5

*"Open up, Esther Jean Wagner!" Clancy Kelly pounded on the front door of the large house. "We know you're in there! You open up right this second!"*

*Clancy, Darby, and their son, Aiden, all stood on the front porch of Esther Jean Wagner's house, red-faced and angry, ready for a fight. They had allowed things to go on for as long as possible, but their patience was running thin. Robbie was nearly sixteen-years-old. Everyone was getting anxious, fearful that the day would come that it was too late to enact the plan. Esther Jean Wagner needed to do as she said and stop pussyfootin' around about it. The boy had to go—one way or another. The Kellys had a new plan of their own. They weren't going to wait for Robbie to go away. They'd take care of him themselves.*

*All three of the Kellys jumped back as the door finally swung wide, revealing Esther Jean Wagner, still in her bib overalls, plaid farmer's shirt, and gardening clogs, her arms crossed under her breast. The Kellys, filled with piss and vinegar only moments prior, found themselves inching backward on the porch, putting more space between the open door and themselves. Esther Jean Wagner merely glared out at the three of them and their shotguns, not looking the least bit concerned by the firepower they had brought with them.*

*"What are you fools doin' on my damn property?" Esther Jean Wagner barked. "Robbie's in bed. If you wake him up—"*

*"We're here for the boy." Clancy Kelly managed to choke out, though the crack in his voice betrayed him.*

*"That so?" Esther Jean's eyebrow raised precipitously.*

*"Give us the boy, Mrs. Wagner." The Kelly's eldest commanded in a voice no more authoritative or confident than his father's. "Give us Robbie, and we can have this all done with once and for all."*

*Esther Jean chuckled.*

*"You think that's gonna stop anything, ya' damn idjit?" She asked, her eyes boring into each of the Kellys eyes in turn. "You're just gonna do away with him, and then you ain't gotta worry no more?"*

*"That's about right." Mr. Kelly glanced at his wife, whose eyes were fixed on the floorboards of the porch, afraid to look up. "We're tired of this nonsense. We want to end it once and for all."*

*"He's the last." Esther Jean's eyes shot over to Clancy. "There ain't no more after him. You ain't even givin' him no chance to have any kids his own. There might be a distant relative, I supposed, but if you kill him—"*

*"Then we're rid of this curse!" The eldest son of the Kelly's barked, a little braver than he had been.*

*"You are the dumbest sonsabitches I ever had the bad fortune to look at in my life. Ugliest, too. If there was an award ceremony for stupid, you'd sweep the whole damn thing." Esther Jean leveled them with her eyes. "He's comin' back one way or another. Somehow or some way. If you get rid of the boy, ain't no one savin' your sorry asses then. We'll all be up Shit Creek without a paddle in a glass-bottomed boat."*

*"We got a chance to end this for good, Esther Jean." Mr. Kelly pled with her, no longer angry, simply lost for other solutions. "I don't like it none—"*

*"I think it's time for you, Clancy. Darby. Y'all need to retire down to Florida." Esther Jean stated evenly, her pupils dilating until her irises disappeared into a black hole. "Get away from things."*

*All three Kellys stiffened as their eyes locked onto Esther Jean Wagner's.*

*"And you should just forget this ever happened, Aiden." She addressed their eldest son. "That'll get us right back on track."*

*All three Kellys slowly nodded.*

*"We can't leave." Mr. Kelly seemed to have a thought, his voice pouring forth from his lips robotically. "He'll never let us leave."*

*"Well," Esther Jean fluttered a hand in the air as if this meant nothing to her, "you're just goin' for an extended vacation. You ain't tryin' to escape, is ya'? So what if it's a really long damn vacation? You drive on out of town feeling like you plan on comin' back sometime in the future. But...don't."*

*Again, all three of the Kellys nodded along.*

*"Now," Esther Jean Wagner's irises emerged from the black hole of their pupils, "y'all get your pug-ugly asses off my porch, ya' hear?"*

*The Kellys all shook their heads as if coming out of a dream.*

*"I don't want to see none of y'all on my property ever again!" Esther Jean warned them. "If I do, I'll be the one using a shotgun, damnit. That's a damn promise."*

*The door of the big house was slammed in the three adults' faces. Mr. and Mrs. Kelly looked at each other, confused for a moment, then turned to walk away. Aiden, their eldest, simply fell in behind them.*

"All she's done is lie to me. To us." I muttered under my breath. "I can't trust her. She's not my grandmother."

"Babe," Lucas reached over, his hand landing on my thigh gently, his fingers giving the flesh there a squeeze, "no offense, but what other bright ideas do you have?"

"I don't."

"Exactly." He nodded firmly. "Who else is going to help us now?"

"How about," I searched my brain for the name of anyone other than the woman claiming to be my grandmother but wasn't, "Carlita?"

"We can't get out of Point Worth." Lucas frowned at me. "How are we going to get to Toledo to get help from her? And why did you think of her anyway, babe?"

"She's an oracle." I shrugged impishly.

"Good information to have had a while back." Lucas' frown deepened.

"Sorry."

Lucas shrugged. "Doesn't matter much now."

"How about Mr. Barkley?" I asked quickly. "Surely your grandfather knows something about—"

"Really?" Lucas snorted. "You think grandpa can protect us from anything? Can he fix our memories, babe?"

"Well, no..."

"Exactly. We have to see Esther Jean, Rob."

"No."

"Why not?" Lucas groaned. "I know you don't trust her, but it's not like we have any real friends left, Rob. We have to trust someone, even if it's a little foolish. Someone has to help us, and she's the only one I know with magic and maybe some information."

"I wish the book had been some kind of help."

"A storybook isn't going to help us, Rob."

"I know."

"So?"

"Look," I turned to look at Lucas, "Esther Jean Wagner—if that's even her real name—is a goddamn liar, Lucas. Suddenly, the other night, it just really sunk in. I didn't know her before my parents disappeared to...wherever they disappeared to, okay? Hell. She could have been the person who made them disappear for all I know. Especially with my lapse in memory here. Regardless of why my parents are gone, where they went to, if she had anything to do with it—I don't have any memories of her before they disappeared. It also makes me question everything about whether or not she has anything to do with our memory problems because..."

"Because what?"

"If she fucked with our memories, why didn't she just give me some fake memories about her when I was a small child?" I shrugged. "I mean, that's a real lapse of judgment on her part, right?"

"I suppose..."

"One day, some weird shit went down at the house. I was a small child. My mom was making breakfast in the kitchen, and shit...just went down. And she was gone. I don't know anything more than that to tell you. Then I remember my dad tucking me into bed that night. Then he was gone in the morning, and this...person...showed up and said she was my grandmother. I can remember that now. I came downstairs because someone was knocking on the door. It was that...*woman*...and when I asked her who she was, she said she was my grandmother. *I remember that now.* But I don't have any memory of her before that moment. If she was really my grandmother, I would have some sort of memory of her at Christmas or Thanksgiving...or a family reunion or talking to her on the phone during the holidays at the least. But...nothing, Lucas. She didn't exist to me before that moment."

"That's crazy."

"I'm not crazy!" I barked.

Lucas smiled gently at me.

"I meant that the situation is crazy." He squeezed my thigh again. "Not you, babe."

"Oh."

"I'm on your side, remember?" He reminded me. "We're a team."

"Yeah." I sighed as I laid my hand on his, letting our fingers intertwine. "Sorry. I'm kind of on edge here."

"I don't know why." Lucas teased.

Darkness was creeping in on all sides of the car. The woods around us were deathly silent, making our low voices sound like we were giving commencement speeches in a huge auditorium. At least, that's what it felt like. When a person is scared that they might be drawing attention to themselves, every little noise they make sounds amplified.

"Everything she has told me is a lie." I reiterated. "Well, maybe not every little thing. No one can lie about absolutely everything. But the important stuff was all lies. She knows what happened to my parents. She knows I'm not her grandson. She did something to our memories—just like you said—I believe that to be true. And she has something to do with all of this shit going on around us. We can't trust her."

"Do you think we can't trust her to tell the truth, or we can't trust her to keep us safe?"

"What's the difference?" I let go of Lucas' hand and turned to look out my window into the darkness. "Trust is trust. If you can't trust a person, you don't know if they'll sell you up the river the first chance they get. How do we know she won't help us until the man in the black hooded cloak shows up, Lucas? Then she just...tosses us to the wolves. No pun intended."

"Surely." Lucas snorted and pulled my hand back into his. "What other option do we have, though? That's my whole argument. We can drive around Point Worth until you run out of gas—which, by the way, we're running dangerously low on—or the sun comes up, whichever is first. Or we can go see if your—Esther Jean Wagner can help."

"How do we know she won't just attack us when we show up?"

"I don't."

"If she starts a fight, I'm not so sure I can take her, babe." I sighed. "She could easily kill us both. I mean, maybe. Sometimes she acts scared of me. Like she's afraid I'll blast her to smithereens or something…but other times…she's kind of formidable."

Lucas laughed.

"Yeah." He said. "I've seen those looks she gets."

I couldn't help but chuckle.

"Rob," He sighed, "just one last point I can make here. She kept you alive until you decided to leave town, and—"

"Which she probably put into my head!"

"—and if she wanted to do you harm, don't you think she would have done it when you were young and defenseless? When you didn't know how to use your magic?"

"I don't remember, Lucas," I grumbled. "Forget that part? Maybe she did try in the past and wasn't able? I don't have any idea what might have happened between us before I ran off. Which, I can't even remember why I really decided to do that."

"We decided that you should leave," Lucas said suddenly. "You and I."

"What?"

"You and I made that decision," Lucas stated, his eyes darting around as if trying to remember something. "Maybe Esther Jean had something to do with that, but—"

"Is that something you just know again?" I urged him on.

"No, Rob." Lucas turned to me, his eyes suddenly focused. "I just remembered that."

I just stared at him.

"Why are we getting glimpses of memories we didn't have before?" Lucas asked hurriedly. "Every now and then, I'm getting memories I didn't have…minutes ago. What is that about? Is Esther Jean still messing with us somehow? Is that a real memory? Is it fake? What's going on, babe?"

Chewing at my lip, I thought about that.

"You said something is draining magic out of Point Worth?" I began.

"Yeah?"

"Maybe whatever was keeping us in this...*fog*...is being stripped away, too." I suggested warily. "If we wait long enough..."

"We'll remember everything?" Lucas finished for me. "Like...remember the actual truth?"

"Maybe?"

Lucas continued to stare at me, as if processing that thought, working it over in his brain from beginning to end. Testing out the strength of such a theory before he settled on believing it to be true.

"Okay," I said. "Okay. Okay. So...I'm the only person in this town whose magic isn't tied to him, right?"

"Okay. Sure."

"Say the magic is tied to this land. To Point Worth. He's been siphoning off the land over the years...however many years he's been trapped—"

"I think he's been around a really long time, babe." Lucas shivered.

"Right." I nodded. "He's been siphoning it and parceling it out. Preparing for...I don't know. His return?"

"Okay. I can follow that."

"Now he's sucking it all back up. He's loading up for bear, Lucas."

"Are you the bear?" Lucas whispered.

"Obviously." I shrugged, then shivered involuntarily. "I just don't know why I'm a bear. I'm barely...*anything*. But, without my memories,

I have no clue if I know the answer to that stuck somewhere in the deep corners of my mind or not. Maybe I do know...I just can't remember?"

"We have to see Esther Jean," Lucas stated firmly. "If she's losing her magic, too—"

"She said the other day that the Kobolds disappeared because..."

"Because why?"

"She made it sound like it was because I had jumped in the well and used up the magic that was left there," I said quickly. "Maybe that was a reservoir of some kind that only people in my family could get to...or maybe they disappeared because he's been draining magic for years now. The magic in the well was the only thing keeping them from being...*sucked up*...too?"

"That makes a little sense," Lucas said, then grumbled. "I wish I had my freaking memories. The real ones."

I nodded along. "But Oma—Esther Jean—said there was no point in planting the garden anymore. I'm not sure why she ever started planting it—I don't have a memory of the first time she planted it—but maybe she meant that the magic in the land was getting sucked up and the garden wouldn't thrive anyway. If that makes sense?"

"A little."

My eyes met Lucas'.

"He's definitely planning something big, babe."

"Let's see Esther Jean," Lucas repeated. "Let's go."

Sighing, I reached for the keys in the ignition. Pausing, I turned my head to look into Lucas' eyes again.

“If she kills me, you, or both of us, I’m going to be very pissed at you.” I winked, though my stomach was like lead.

“Well, we can argue about it in Hell.” Lucas chuckled nervously.

“Why wouldn’t we go to Heaven?” I laughed as I started the car.

“No one is going to let two perverts like us past the Pearly Gates, babe,” Lucas replied as he fastened his seatbelt.

“God loves the gays.” I admonished him playfully as I put the car into reverse and eased up off of the brake. “He gave us Matt Bomer and Luke Evans.”

“And another certain gay, hunky movie star.” Lucas reached over to pinch my cheek as I laughed and started backing up.

# Chapter 6

The Sunny Side-Up Café had flames licking up the north wall, inching towards the roof. The modest, yet beautiful, bushes out front were already skeletal candles, their flames licking towards the sky. Before long, the flames would be crawling over every inch of the café, devouring it from the outside in, until it was nothing more than a shell. The crack that ran down the center of Main Street was more than wide enough for a grown man to dive into, splitting the town of Point Worth from South to North. When the sun started to rise over the eastern horizon, night and day would meet at the center of town, and only one would win the battle.

Carlita held her hand out before her, focusing on the crack, doing her best to use what magics she had left to slow the widening of the chasm. Jackson Barkley still stood to her side, watching nervously as the ground rumbled beneath their feet, yet the crack didn't grow wider. Andrew was chewing at his lip on Carlita's other side, watching with the same level of anxiety as Jackson Barkley, wondering if Carlita could hold out long enough. Ever composed, Carlita's face was an impassive mask as she focused on the task before her. All she had to do was give Rob, Lucas, and Esther Jean just enough time to figure out a plan.

Deep in her mind, Carlita knew that Rob and Lucas had made a decision—one that neither of them quite understood yet. Carlita also knew that Esther Jean was aware and was preparing for their arrival. Beyond that, Carlita had no idea what was to come, which was a strange experience for an oracle. Carlita had lived her very long life always one step ahead of the game, knowing where she had to be, when she needed to be there, and why she needed to do the things she did. Aside from doing everything in her limited magical power to keep the crack in Main Street from spreading, she knew only one other thing.

*And she was prepared for that if nothing else.*

"Carlita," Jackson grumbled nervously.

"Yes, honey?" She responded simply, as though the work she was doing wasn't testing her down to her bones.

"There's no way you can hold it together forever." He said gently.

"Well," Carlita answered, "I don't have to, do I?"

"This is crazy." Andrew spat, though he didn't move to run away or abandon his friends.

"Well, if there was money in stating the obvious, you'd be able to take us all to the Bahamas, baby." Carlita turned her head to wink at him.

Beads of sweat were appearing on her brow, though her smile didn't falter. Andrew shook his head, but a smile came to his face. The ground stopped rumbling, but only for the briefest of moments, which took all three of them by surprise. Carlita frowned and turned to look at the crack in Main Street. Slowly, she pulled back on her magic and lowered her arm. Steam still continued to rise from the crack, but the ground was still, and the crack didn't suddenly split open before them. Jackson shifted nervously from foot to foot as Carlita and Andrew both stared down at the crevice before them.

"Well," Carlita mumbled, "I guess we just have to wait and—"

"Carlita!" Andrew gasped, his hand reaching out to squeeze her forearm.

"What?" She replied in unison with Jackson.

"Shit." Andrew hissed.

Carlita looked over at Andrew, to find him staring off towards the east end of Main Street. Jackson followed suit, his eyes traveling from the crack and over to Andrew. When they saw the fear in their friend's eyes, and where he was looking, their heads turned in unison to search out whatever he had seen. At the east end of Main Street, two wolves were standing shoulder to shoulder, red eyes glowing in the darkness at the end of the street that the flames—which were licking up the side of The Sunny Side-Up Café—did not cast light on yet. Both wolves' fangs were on display as they growled at the threesome at the other end of the crevice on Main Street.

"I'm surprised," Carlita stated blandly, turning her head to look at her friends in turn. "Are you surprised?"

"Carlita." Jackson whimpered, shifting more as he stood beside her.

"Goddamnit." Andrew hissed.

"Jackson Barkley," Carlita stated with finality. "I think it's time you go on into the hardware store, don't you? Give Esther Jean a call."

"Wuh-what?" Jackson stammered.

"Let her know she doesn't have much time, would you?" Carlita nudged him. "Go on now. Get out of the way. You got other things you need to be doing."

Jackson stared into Carlita's eyes for a few moments, as though unsure if he should listen or not. Would he be cowardly for abandoning his friends in their time of need—to make a phone call?

The ground began rumbling again, and the crack spread another inch. Steam exploded in bursts from deep within.

"Well?" Carlita nudged him harder. "Go. Tell Esther Jean to be ready, Jackson. Only you can do this."

"Right." Jackson nodded shakily. "Okay. Yeah."

When he showed no actual intention of moving, Carlita smiled warmly and reached for his hand. She gave it a gentle squeeze.

"My friend." She said. "You've done well. For your part."

A single tear slid down Jackson's cheek.

"I didn't really expect this to happen, ya' know?" Jackson shook his head.

"Well, I wish I could say I had your same confidence." Carlita chuckled. "Now go. Please."

Jackson nodded once, and then he was sprinting towards his hardware store as fast as his legs allowed. Carlita sighed as she watched him go, knowing she would never see the man again.

"Baby," Carlita turned to Andrew, "it's your time to shine."

"Right." Andrew didn't look at her.

His eyes were on the wolves at the other end of the street.

"Don't let me down," Carlita stated as she raised her hand towards the crack once more.

As magic poured forth in a column from Carlita's hand towards the growing crevice, and the ground shook underfoot, Andrew fell to all fours. A ripple of magic coursed through the air, and Andrew's body started to shift. The wolves at the end of the street leaned their heads back, fangs still showing as they howled up at the moon. The flames from The Sunny Side-Up Care shot into the air, roaring with fury as Andrew's skin violently split, sending fluids and sinew flying as he spontaneously turned. Carlita ignored the splatter of liquid against her side as she focused on the crack in the street.

Then two wolves charged west. Another wolf charged east to meet them.

The ground shook.

A low cackle carried on the wind.

"*That's what she said, Esther Jean.*" Jackson Barkley's voice was shaky over the static-y line.

Esther Jean stood in the kitchen, holding the large phone receiver to her ear. The only landline in the house had always hung just inside the kitchen next to the door that led to the cellar. Why Jackson Barkley hadn't bothered calling her on her cellphone was beyond her, but Esther Jean knew the call was important, regardless of the method of delivery. Cell service was probably down anyway. At least in Point Worth. She slid one hand into the pocket of her bib overalls and leaned her shoulder against the wall as she stared out at nothing.

"Well, I guess you'd have no reason to lie to me." She sighed into the receiver, wondering if the static would make it difficult for Jackson to understand her. "What's goin' on there?"

"*Are you fuckin' crazy, Esther Jean Wagner?*" Jackson barked, though humor slipped into his tone. "*Carlita's doin' all she can to keep this town from turnin' into one big sinkhole and Andrew's off fightin' pack. And you want to know how we're doin'? If my own long-departed wife rose from the grave, walked up in here, and took a shit on the check-out counter, I wouldn't be the least bit surprised. How's that for how we're doin'?*"

"That's about how I figured it was goin'." Esther Jean sighed. "All right. Well, y'all keep doin' the best you can. I got pots on every fire over here, too."

"*I'm sure you do,*" Jackson grumbled in disbelief. "*Probably sipping iced tea and waitin' on the boys to show up.*"

"Well, that's my lot in life, ya' old bastard."

"*I never did like you.*"

"Well," Esther Jean waggled her head, though there was no one to see it anymore, "you didn't have trouble liking me a few times after Betty Lynn died to get away from ya'."

Even with everything happening on Main Street, Jackson Barkley's laughter carried across the line to the receiver in her hand.

"*I'll miss the good times, that's for sure.*" Jackson sniffed. "*Esther Jean?*"

"What, bastard?"

*"Tell my grandson I love him. Might not get a chance myself."*

"I'll do it. Twice." Esther Jean nodded firmly. "Tell Carlita, if you get the chance, that I'll make sure she didn't fight for nothin'. Ya' hear me?"

*"All right,"* Jackson answered. *"And Esther Jean?"*

"Yeah?" She barked, feigning annoyance.

But the line went dead.

The ground beneath the house rumbled gently, if "gentle" was ever a way to describe the movement from below. Sighing to herself, Esther Jean returned the receiver to its cradle smoothly. Just as quickly as it had started, the rumbling beneath the house stopped. She wanted to believe that maybe a miracle had occurred, but she knew better. It wouldn't be long before the ground was shaking again. When it did, it would be a shake to end all shakes. Esther Jean shuffled over wearily, her arms and legs feeling like lead, and grabbed her glass of tea off of the kitchen table. She looked around the kitchen one last time, then exited the kitchen, making her way to the front door.

When she exited the house, she didn't bother shutting the door behind herself. Anything that would want in the house would have no trouble finding its way in, closed doors and windows be damned. There was no protecting herself or her home any longer, so why bother pretending otherwise? Esther Jean shuffled out onto the porch, her legs pulling downwards, as if trying to send her into the Earth. She ignored the sensation, having felt it dozens, if not hundreds of times over the years—just never this strongly.

Instead, she shuffled over to a chair and eased herself down.

Bringing the glass of tea to her lips, she took a sip. Licking her lips, she lowered the glass to the arm of the chair, cradling it in her hand there.

"Now," She looked out over her property into the thickening darkness that was slowly making the stars and moon blink out, "where the hell are them boys at?"

Lucas felt like a livewire next to me, the way he was shifting and shimmying in the passenger seat of the car as it idled at the opening to the driveway. The drive from the wooded area where we had parked, a few miles from Lucas' house on the shore of Lake Erie, to Oma's house had felt…different. Although I'd made the drive dozens of times over the last few weeks, the drive felt longer this time. But also, shorter. Lucas had remained silent the entire time, and I had nothing to distract me from the sense of impending doom permeating every fiber of my being. I both wanted to find someone to help us, yet I didn't want to see Oma. In my heart of hearts, I knew she wasn't my grandmother. I knew she had done nothing but lie and deceive me for my entire life. The reasons were completely unknown to me, and I wasn't sure I'd understand even if I had all of my memories back.

With the silence of Lucas making the ride tense, not wanting to see Oma, but also concerned about finding anyone who could help us with our problem, the ride felt both torturously slow and fretfully fast. As we sat at the end of the driveway, the car in Drive but my foot on the brake, I couldn't help but feel that it was darker outside than usual. The darkness that surrounded us out on the old road that led to the lake and Oma's house felt almost tangible. As if something was closing in around us, crushing down upon us.

Somewhere, in the furthest reaches of my brain, I knew that it wasn't just my imagination that the darkness was thicker and blacker than usual for no reason. The man in the black hooded cloak was coming, and that was affecting everything in Point Worth. If we were right in our hypothesis about what was going on in our little hometown, that made a lot of sense. He was draining everything from the land, all of the magic that made it what it was. He was siphoning off everything that was good and pure—even any source of light that chased away bad things.

Eventually, as the night wore on, I imagined Point Worth would look like *The Void* in *Stranger Things*. Nothing but inky blackness surrounding us, leaving us able to only see houses and people—no detail or light to the world. Just stuff. Stuff that the man in the black hooded cloak would eventually wipe away, just like he had done in my dreams. Nothing could prepare a person for what I knew he had in mind for Point Worth—and probably, eventually, the world—but I knew what those plans were. My mind couldn't even hold such an idea or wrap itself around an idea like that. Nothing but eternal dark and nothingness, with only him left. He would devour everything with his power, growing more and more hungry for power until he left the Earth nothing more than a black hole that no light escaped.

"What are we waiting on?" Lucas asked softly, his hand reaching for and squeezing my thigh once again. "Sitting here is just making this worse, babe."

"I know," I said, though my foot stayed on the brake pedal. "I'm just working myself up to doing this, ya' know."

"Rip the bandage off, Rob." He patted my thigh. "It'll be easier."

I looked over at him. He smiled.

"Promise." He reassured me. "And I'm here with you."

"No matter what?"

"No matter what." He leaned over and gave me a lingering kiss that never could have lasted long enough.

As Lucas pulled away, a smile on his face, I allowed myself a happy sigh, then I eased off of the brake and moved my foot to the gas. Inch by inch, we eased down the driveway, on our way to Oma's house. As we drove along, Lucas kept his hand on my thigh for reassurance, squeezing the flesh there to remind me that I wasn't alone. No matter what we found at Oma's house, we would find it together. Even though Oma's house was settled quite a way off of the road that led to the lake, we would have seen any flames if it had been on fire. A house as big as hers doesn't burn without letting the whole county know, so I knew that the wolves had not come and played pyromaniacs. However, the fact that the house was not on fire concerned me. Had they shown up but hadn't done anything to give it away? Were they lying in wait for us on Oma's property somewhere?

The thought made me nearly slam on the brake and throw the car into reverse, but my mind told me that there was nowhere to hide. If they were at Oma's, we might as well face the wolves, too. We'd eventually run into them somewhere. We couldn't leave Point Worth—not as a pair—and I wouldn't leave alone—and the darkness was closing in around us. There was no way we could luck out and not run into them before morning came. As we got to the far end of the driveway, Oma's house came into view in the clearing. It was funny to me that not even a month before, I had been elated to see the old house. Now, it made my stomach flip-flop in my gut.

Oma was on the porch, sitting there, drinking a glass of tea like the world wasn't burning down around her. That did nothing to make my gut feel better. Lucas gave my thigh another squeeze as I continued pulling up to the house, only stopping when I was within ten feet of it. I looked through the windshield at Oma, and she raised the glass in a salute and then took another sip, calm as you please. Of course, she had been waiting for us. Why should I have expected anything different?

# Chapter 7

*He was so strange, the boy with dark hair and eyes. Unlike the other boys in the Point Worth Regional Middle School, he didn't try to prove himself with bravado, bullying, or bragging behaviors. Carrying himself with confidence, or what could have been complete obliviousness in other's opinions, he was hard not to notice. He didn't pay attention to rude comments, nor did he seem to puff up when complimented. Like a self-sustaining organism found in the furthest reaches of the world, he needed no one and required nothing from anyone. He was an island. It made the other boys both angry and envious, emotions they were not mature enough to handle at such an age. It made the girls equally enamored and annoyed. The boy never took notice of either.*

*Lucas found himself staring at the boy during every class that they shared at the middle school. He'd watch the way the boy sat up, paying attention to the teachers, not caring if this made him look like a nerd. Lucas watched the way the boy sat back in his chair with ease and stared off at nothing when he was bored, unconcerned with teachers catching him. It wasn't rebellious behavior on the boy's part, the drifting off into daydreams—just starry-eyed childhood daydreaming to which all boys that age are prone. At lunch, the boy moved through the line with his tray, easily making conversation with other kids, even the ones he wasn't friends with, able to sit down and eat with any group he wished. Even if he sat down with a group of kids who didn't like him, by the end of their shared meal, the kids seemed to have changed their minds about him.*

*Robbie.*

*His name was Robbie. But he preferred "Rob."*

*Quick to make a joke that anyone could enjoy. Generous with compliments and positive words for all. Rob was one of Lucas' favorite people. But Rob had no idea. Just the sight of Rob passing in the hall and flashing his pearly whites made Lucas' tummy flip-flop, though he had no idea what that meant at such a young age.*

*Lucas could remember the first time he saw Rob walk into the first class they shared that year. He had already been in his seat, looking for someone he kind of knew in the class to become quick friends with, so he wouldn't feel like a nerd, when Rob entered, backpack slung over his shoulder in a Devil-may-care sort of way. When Lucas looked up, Rob's head slowly turned, as if from some slow-motion scene in a teen movie, and their eyes met.*

*Lightning.*

*Electricity shot through Lucas' body, and he had to avert his eyes from Rob's. Something had traveled through his body, shook him to his core, grabbed ahold of the innermost part of him that he didn't even have a name for, and turned his world upside down. When Lucas looked up again, Rob was looking away, seemingly unaware of what had just transpired in Lucas' soul. Finally, Rob made his way to a seat across the room from Lucas. However, before he sat down at his desk, his eyes flashed over to Lucas once more.*

*He looked...shaken.*

*Rob looked shaken. Someone like Rob could be unnerved.*

*It was then that Lucas knew something had been set in motion. He just didn't know what that thing was.*

"Well," Oma swiped her hand over the arm of her chair, brushing away imaginary dust as we stood at the base of the steps up to the porch, "you boys took your time gettin' over here, didn't ya'?"

"Hi, Oma," I replied blandly.

She considered me for a moment as Lucas' head turned from mine to hers, then back again, watching our transaction with rapt attention.

"Couldn't get out, could ya'?"

"We're standing here, aren't we?" I snapped.

"Well," Oma sniffed haughtily, "maybe you just had a change of heart, smart ass. How the fuck would I know?"

"Because no one's been fucking with your brain." I tapped my temple with an index finger violently as I snarled up at her. "That's how, old woman."

"Wuh-hell. Someone's pissy." Oma waggled her head down at me before bringing the tea to her lips and taking a sip. "Someone tell ya' that even the gays don't look good in body glitter?"

Before I could snarl back some equally hateful retort, Lucas' fingers wrapped around my wrist, stopping me.

"Mrs. Wagner." Lucas piped up. "I've never been disrespectful to you."

"Ya' haven't." She nodded.

"But, we're here to tell you to stop messing with our memories," Lucas said. "Whatever you've done, we need you to undo it. Now. And we need answers."

"Ask wise ass over here." Oma gestured at me rudely. "He knows fuckin' everything, doesn't he? Speaking of which—you're so damn smart all of the damn sudden, why the hell did you not just stay gone, Robbie? Why didn't you leave as soon as Andrew tried attacking you? You're so damn smart, but every damn thing that's gone wrong has made you make one bad decision after another. Instead of runnin' tail and getting' away from danger, you just dive in headfirst like a grade-A village idiot. Point Worth's collective I.Q. went down a few digits since you came back. And it wasn't that high to begin with."

"You miserable old—" I began.

"Ya' just couldn't stay gone, could ya'?" She interjected. "You got out of town, and things was fine. Things would-a stayed fine a lot longer if you had just done as you was supposed to. But, like always, you had to do things your way. Here we are, Robbie. Good job!"

Lucas was squeezing my wrist tightly, so I kept my mouth shut.

"Why was he supposed to stay gone?" Lucas asked evenly, though I could hear in his voice, and feel in his grip, how tense he was.

"You boys may not got your memories," Oma crossed her arms over her chest as she turned her head to look at him, "but it doesn't take memories to figure out what's going on here, does it? This town is about to be swallowed up.

He's comin' for ya'. And he shouldn't've been comin' for another few decades. That was the damn plan anyway—if wiseass over there had just stuck to the plan. I suppose it just is what it is. He's comin'. Bloody Bones is comin' for ya'."

As she said the last sentence, her eyes turned to me. A shiver ran up my spine as Oma said the name of the man in the black hooded cloak. A name we had sworn we would never say out loud again...unless it wouldn't matter either way. Her saying his name out loud confirmed my theory that he really was returning; otherwise she never would have said his name like that, out in the open, with not a care in the world. Lucas' hand fell away from my wrist immediately, and he gasped, obviously recognizing the name. In the deepest recesses of his mind, that name had been hidden away. Hearing it out loud had startled him.

"He's comin' for you, Robbie." Oma jabbed a finger at me. "Just like you've always known—when your head wasn't all clusterfucked. And he's going to pull Point Worth down to Hell in the process."

"There's access to Hell in Point Worth, Ohio," I stated blandly. "I'd like to say I'm shocked, but—"

"You can keep being a smartass all you want." Oma snapped. "But this is your damn fault."

"How?" I snapped back. "How is any of this my damn fault? I don't even remember everything except who he is and that he's trouble. Or the things you want me to think I remember. Well, that, and you're not my grandmother, you crazy old bitch!"

Oma's fists went to her hips, and her face turned up in a sneer as she leaned forward to launch in on me once more.

"Wait." Lucas jumped in before she could say another word. "You're not his grandmother. Buh-loody Bones is coming. We don't have our memories. You're blaming Rob for everything. Mrs. Wagner...you have explaining to do. None of this makes any sense whatsoever."

"Took the words out of my mouth," I mumbled.

"Shut up, wise-ass!" Oma snapped.

"Are you going to help us or what?" I snapped back.

"Of course, I am, ya' damn fool!" Oma threw her hands up in the air. "That's what I'm here to do. I was just expecting to do it twenty years from now. When you wasn't such a damn pup and completely unprepared for what's to come. In all my years—"

"You'd think you'd have learned some patience and decorum?" I quipped.

"Rob," Lucas mumbled.

"Well, if you're going to keep bein' sassy with me, then I won't give a damn if—"

Before Oma could finish her sentence, the ground began to rumble beneath us. A low roar met our ears as the three of us did our best to not be knocked over. The rumbling and shaking turned into what I could only compare to all of the earthquakes I'd witnessed while in California. The only problem was, *we weren't in California.* We were smackdab in the middle of the buttcrack of Ohio. Earthquakes that can be felt like what we were experiencing was not common in Ohio. Lucas and I grabbed onto each other as the shaking under our feet intensified and off in the distance, a boom that was probably deafening if a person was nearby, sounded.

Just as quickly as the shaking started, it stopped. Glancing up at the porch as I held onto Lucas, just in case the ground started shaking once more, I saw that Oma had her hand braced against the porch railing, but she had remained on her feet. She looked drained. Not physically—something else. After a second, I realized that Bloody Bones siphoning off magic was doing a number on her as well. I couldn't help but wonder if that meant that she was losing her powers or if she was just experiencing side effects of such a perversion of nature. Slowly, Lucas and I slid our arms from around each other and stood tall, looking up at Oma as she let go of the railing and faced us.

"Well, shit." Oma spat. "I guess we gotta stop chewing each other new assholes and get down to business, don't we?"

"I'd say so," Lucas answered for us.

# Chapter 8

Carlita was sprawled on the asphalt, legs splayed, and only her hands behind her holding her up into a half-seated position. Blood trickled from the corner of her mouth and from both nostrils, the result of the large pieces of shrapnel from the explosion. Bloody Bones had broken free. Smoke, almost like a dense, soup-like fog, hung lazily along the crack dividing Main Street, obscuring Carlita's view of what had risen. Smiling bitterly, Carlita turned her head to the side and spat, a rivulet of red splattering against the black road. She held herself up with one arm while she used the back of her other arm to wipe her mouth partially clean. Whether she liked it or not—and she hated admitting defeat—her end had come. She turned her eyes to look out at where the explosion had come from the crack in the street.

Bit by bit, the smoke laying like a haze on Main Street began to dissipate. At first, he was nothing more than a shadow in the haze, but as more of the smoke cleared away, Carlita could see him more clearly. The black of his cloak intensified, the outline of his hood became sharper. Bloody Bones stood next to the large hole in the center of Main Street, the large crack running in either direction away from it. Carlita didn't bother to rise to her feet since one only rises to greet someone they respect. She stayed there on the ground, watching as Bloody Bones raised his head and bright red eyes, and gleaming teeth peered out at her.

Carlita sighed, shaking her head at the sight.

She didn't want to be resigned to the fact that he had risen—yet again—but looking into the depths of his hood, her eyes meeting his, there was no denying the fact. He was back.

Bloody Bones walked casually towards her, the bottom of his cloak rustling in the breeze, sweeping away lingering smoke in wisps as he approached.

"We meet again, Oracle." Bloody Bones chuckled deeply, warmly, as if greeting an old friend. Of course, Carlita and Bloody Bones had known each other for a long time—but they were not friends. "You haven't aged a day."

He stopped before her, barely the length of a dining table between them.

"Well, you look like shit." Carlita shrugged, then coughed.

More blood.

Bloody Bones cackled.

At the far end of the street, Andrew stood on all fours next to a fallen, headless werewolf, the other werewolf's neck clasped tightly between his teeth.

"You did your very best for a very long time, old friend." Bloody Bones spoke. "But, inevitably, you failed."

"Friend?" Carlita snorted, blood dribbling from her nose as she ignored the pain in her side. "Honey, I give my friends rides to the airport. I wouldn't take you to the corner store."

Bloody Bones raised his arm.

A flash of light.

And Carlita fell back against the street, her skull making a sickening crunching noise against the asphalt.

Her eyes were open, but she saw nothing.

Andrew, in his wolf form, stared in horror as the werewolf in his grasp thrashed, trying to get away. With a quick jerk, Andrew tore the throat of the other werewolf, then let him drop to the street. He stared at the scene at the other end of Main Street, horrified at the death of Carlita. If she was dead...

There was only one thing to do.

He turned on all four legs and ran as quickly as he could, one of his legs hurt and refusing to work right.

There was only one place that was safe now.

If only he could get there on his hurt leg.

Bloody Bones smiled wickedly down at his first real kill since freeing himself from his prison, his red eyes and white fangs gleaming down at the oracle who was no more. Sharply, he tilted his head back and howled, summoning his wolves. He howled until he heard the answer of howls in the distance. Soon, they would come. And he could continue his quest. In the meantime...

Bloody Bones turned, his cloak dancing around him as he turned towards Barkley's Hardware. He had one more score to settle. Swiftly, without a second thought, he glided across the street and through the door of the old man's shop.

Moments later, Jackson Barkley's screams pealed through the air.

Then Main Street was silent.

Except for the howls of approaching wolves.

*Ibiza was one of my favorite party destinations when I was in the middle of my (possibly—depending upon whom you ask) illustrious career as an international movie and rock star. Off the east coast of Spain, before one gets to Mallorca, Ibiza is a great place to get away from everything that a celebrity would want to get away from at times. There was the good food, the nightlife, other celebrities who understood my pain and troubles, the relaxation—though I did little of that—and the ability to just escape from what my life had become. It was on Ibiza, at a night club, off my head on Ecstasy, that I ran into Shepard Bachman. Horrible name, but also horribly famous.*

*Shepard Bachman, like myself, was an out and proud male actor from Hollywood, there to enjoy all of the hedonism the island had to offer. Possibly more famous than myself, Shepard had a few years on me, as far as careers go, so he'd had more time to work on his stock. He'd starred in more movies—even some of those superhero movies that make a billion dollars worldwide—and had the clout that made everyone desire him. When I had walked into the club with my "friends" and went to the VIP area to sit down at our reserved banquette, people noticed. When Shepard walked into the club, it was like a parting of the Red Sea. People didn't just notice—they were starstruck.*

*One way or another, he had ended up sitting next to me at my table, trading war stories, sipping obscenely expensive cocktails and champagne, laughing like he hadn't a care in the world. Maybe he didn't. I wasn't Shepard. I only knew the troubles of Jacob Michaels. For hours that night, we talked, laughed, drank too many drinks, popped a couple tabs of Ecstasy—the good stuff, none of that crap cut with meth—and danced like we expected the morning to bring about the end of the world. Within hours, pictures of us together would end up on blogs and tabloid sites, even some of the more reputable news sites. However, in those hours together, the world ceased to exist.*

*At the end of the night, in the wee morning hours, as everyone was leaving the club and my handlers were trying to shove me into my waiting vehicle, Shepard had proposed that we carry on the festivities. He could come to my hotel, or I could go to his. As soon as this suggestion met my ears, a vision of green eyes flashed through my mind, and I couldn't think of anything else but how nauseated the thought of sleeping with Shepard Bachman made me. Instead of answering, I merely stared at Shepard as though he was the most disgusting thing I had ever seen, and as the remnants of my Ecstasy induced euphoria coursed through my veins, I allowed my security to shove me into the waiting SUV.*

*As we drove away, Shepard staring after my car quizzically, all I could do was lower my head so that I wouldn't be sick.*

"Fine." Oma shrugged, as though the world wasn't literally falling down around us. "Let's get down to business."

Oma turned to head into the house, as though this one sentence was enough to make us trust her enough to enter the house with her.

"Excuse me." I raised my hand, though her back was turned. "Crazy person? Yeah. You?"

Oma turned to glare at me, her hands going to her hips again.

"Last time I was in that house with you," I reminded her, "you tried to make sure I could never leave again. What on God's green Earth makes you think that I am going to step one foot in that house again?"

"Do ya' think you're safer out here, wise ass?" She asked sharply.

"Rob." Lucas grabbed my hand.

"Hold on, Lucas." I tried to stop him as nicely as possible. "Oma...*Lady*...how do we know that we're safe going in there with you? I don't trust you any further than I can throw you right now."

"Do you feel safe out here?" She barked.

"Absolutely not." I shrugged. "But at least I can see what's coming out here in the open. How do we know you don't have Jason and his wolves in there waiting to jump us? Or Bloody Bones himself."

I felt Lucas shiver next to me, his hand clenching mine tightly.

"Lord," Oma rolled her eyes, her neck rolling back so she could look up to the heavens for guidance, "you'd think with your memory gone, you'd still have common sense, Robbie."

Lucas squeezed my hand, stopping me from answering before he could.

"Meaning what?" He asked quickly.

"Meaning that if I wanted either one of you idiots dead," She waggled her head at us, "you'd be dead. I didn't protect y'all from them idiots of Jason's pack just to have them kill you tonight. And I didn't *fuck with your memories* just to prolong your sufferin'. But if you ain't gonna come in the house like a couple of sensible people, you ain't gonna know nothin' else than what you know right now. You can stand out here until Bloody Bones shows up and kills you both deader than shit. I'll stand here and watch. Might even make me happy to see it, the way you're treatin' me now."

"You just confessed to fucking with our memories, Oma." I snapped at her before Lucas could stop me. "How, exactly, are we the ones treating you poorly?"

"Let it go, Rob." Lucas shook his head.

"Listen to your boyfriend." Oma snorted.

"No." I stammered and pulled my hand out of Lucas'.

Oma watched me as I took a step closer towards the porch and looked up at her. To Lucas' credit, he didn't try to stop me from getting closer to Oma, nor did he tell me to watch what I said to her either. He knew that I had to do what I had to do, so he didn't try to intervene. Bonus points for Lucas. Oma just crossed her arms over her chest again and stared down the steps from her perch a few feet above me as I approached the porch.

"Tell me why you messed with our heads first." I jabbed a finger up at her, making her wince. "Tell me that first. I thought I understood what was going on with why we didn't have our memories—or we didn't have the right memories…or whatever—but now I don't know that I know anything that's correct. I need you to tell me why this is going on before I'll trust you enough to go in that house for even a second, Oma."

"I think that's fair." Lucas sighed from behind me. "And I'd really like to know myself."

Oma sighed, her arms dropping to her sides.

"Because, ya' damn fool," She tried to hiss, but her heart wasn't in it, "I was trying to keep you out of this fight until you had a real chance of winnin' it, wasn't I?"

"How would I know?"

"Well, that's the truth." She nodded firmly. "You forgot a lot of shit because of your own doin'. Not mine. Maybe I put the idea in your head, but it was still your own doin'. But, okay, so I've intervened since you got back. It was obvious that you being back here was undoin' your piddly ass magic and wishes, and something had to be done. I've done all I could to run you back out of this town. You shouldn't be standin' here right now lookin' up at me with all of this sass. You should be off gettin' stronger—just like I thought you would. I figured if we kept you alive a little bit longer, maybe if your magic developed a little bit more—you got a little more mature and less careless—you might live to end up in a nursing home before you hit the grave. But you came back—and it was obvious that threw a wrench in the works. So...I've done what I've had to do to try to get you back on the right path. The one that doesn't end in more death than necessary."

"Well," I shrugged, though I felt chastened for some reason, "Here we are. I'm back, and there's no leaving now. What does that mean?"

"Ask him." Oma jabbed a finger at Lucas. "He's seen it."

Turning to look at Lucas, I could see how pale he had gotten.

"Fire and death, right, Lucas?" Oma asked as I stared at my boyfriend. "You knew wise-ass here was comin' back, and you saw destruction. Tell him. Tell him he's an idiot for returning."

"Lucas?" I whispered.

He just looked up at me, all of the color drained from his face.

"Is that true?" I asked quietly.

"I saw a possibility, Rob." He stated softly. "That's all. I don't see absolutes. Anything can change, I guess."

Oma snorted, and a cackle erupted from her throat. Whipping my head around, I glared up at her.

"What's so funny, asshole?"

"You make wishes, and this one sees possibilities." She shook her head, ruefully. "Shit in one hand and wish in the other—see which one fills up first, why don'tcha?"

"What are you babbling on about now?" I barked.

"Your boyfriend there knows as well as I do that what he's seen is what's to come," Oma stated with finality. "Now it's just a matter of what all that fire and death means. How much fire?

How much death? All we can do now is try to control how far it spreads. We can't stop it."

"Mrs. Wagner." Lucas sighed from behind me. "I didn't specifically see any of you dying. I didn't see anything particular on fire. You're assuming that the destruction I saw involved this town. And us. It could mean *his* destruction."

The fact that Lucas refused to say the name of the man in the black hooded cloak let me know how terrified he was.

"I can't argue that." She relented with a sniff. "But, I still call bullshit."

"Something up here," She tapped her finger against her temple, "told you that Rob was coming back—weeks before even I knew—and it told you that was bad. If the destruction and death you was seeing was Bloody Bones, it wouldn't have filled you with a sense of terror now, would it?"

"Maybe not." Lucas agreed. "But anytime I sense something bad is going to happen, I'm bound to not feel good one way or the other, right?"

"Suppose." She stated simply.

Looking back at Lucas was something I hadn't been able to do as they discussed what Lucas had seen—somewhere in the deep recesses of his mind where his magic worked. Knowing that Lucas knew things that I didn't and not knowing how he decided to interpret them made me uneasy. How did I know if what he saw and how he felt about it was accurate? Even more importantly, I couldn't look and see if my boyfriend was still ashen-faced and uneasy. I didn't want to see the look on his face that told me that he expected doom for us all. Knowing that Bloody Bones was coming was bad enough.

Having it painted all over Lucas' face and seeing how scared that made him was too much.

"So," Oma continued, "I answered your question. We goin' inside or we all gonna sit down for a spell and wait for Bloody Bones to show up and do what he's comin' to do? Y'all's choice."

My mouth desired to spit a few more expletives and insults back and forth with Oma before I even thought about going into her house once again. However, a gust of wind blew in from the direction of Point Worth proper, carrying what could only be the sound of a wolf howling with it. Shivering, I turned to look back at the town in the distance. Of course, all I could see was the vague lights that came from town. Lucas followed my lead, his head turning to look off toward town as well.

Lights, like we were used to seeing, were not what greeted us on the dark horizon. It wasn't large streetlights casting their hazy glow over Point Worth—it was red and yellow flickering light. Like fire. I gasped as Lucas began to shiver. I couldn't help but wonder if Oma hadn't already seen the fire behind us as we fought in front of her porch, yet refused to say anything. Maybe she hadn't wanted us to look back and see for ourselves that what Lucas had seen had come to pass. Was that her trying to distract us from finding out because she had something nefarious in mind...or did she just figure it didn't matter? Was she trying to hide more things from us, or unconcerned with everything now that everything was falling apart?

*Why worry about fire when there're no firemen?*

"Well?" Oma barked, causing Lucas and me to snap our heads back around to look at her.

"Point Worth is on fire," I said simply, my gut slowly traveling towards my knees as I stood there.

"Can't get nothin' past you, can we?" Oma rolled her eyes and turned towards the house.

"Oma?" I whispered.

"Ya' got two choices, Rob," Oma said over her shoulder, pausing for a moment. "Stay out here and watch your hometown burn—and not be able to do anything about it—or get in here, and maybe we can save *something.*"

Then she went into the house. Not another word about me being a wise-ass, no threats, no demands. Oma simply walked into the house, either confident we would follow as she wished, or simply not caring. Of course, with Point Worth on fire, there being no way for Lucas and me to leave Point Worth, and Bloody Bones coming...what else would we do? What else could be done? It truly didn't matter—as far as the town was concerned at that moment—whether or not Lucas and I followed her. So, she was willing to go inside and wait for us to make up our minds one way or another.

"Rob." Lucas sighed from behind me.

I turned to look at him. "Yeah?"

He wasn't ashen-faced or terrified anymore. He just looked sad.

"Get in the car." He said. "There's enough gas to get you out of town. Don't stay here. Maybe you can...I don't know...get far enough away that you'll have time to figure something out? Maybe you can figure out how to do something about...*him*...if you have time. But if you stay here, I'm afraid of what's going to happen."

For the space of several breaths, I stared at Lucas.

"What happens if I don't stay?" I stared into his eyes.

Those green eyes that held nothing but kindness. Now they looked defeated. Resigned. He had accepted something.

"The same thing," He shrugged, "except you won't be one of the casualties."

"Will you?" I asked. "And I can't believe I'm asking this, but will Oma?"

I jabbed a thumb over my shoulder at the house.

"Not that I care." I looked away.

"I only know how this ends if you stay." He whispered.

"Specifically?" My eyebrow raised precipitously.

"Well...I mean, no. Of course not. But there's already fire, and—"

I stepped up to Lucas, silencing him. Doing my best to be reassuring, I smiled and took his face in my hands.

"I'm a fireman," I whispered. "Remember?"

A small smile came to his face.

"Yeah." He nodded. "I said that. Somehow, at the time, I didn't really think this day would come, though, babe."

Looking past him, over his shoulder, I looked off toward town, the red and yellow light showing over the tops of the trees still. In fact, I was pretty sure that the fire was growing. Soon, it might even consume the whole town. Maybe it would work its way to Oma's. It didn't matter.

"The day came." I shrugged dismissively. "I say we go in there, find out what the crazy old lady has to say, and we face this together. Because if I leave—and you stay—and I lose you, there's no way I could face it alone. If I know my final day is coming, I want it to be with you. Okay?"

Lucas nodded. "Okay. I just want you to know that I wouldn't be upset if you ran away. Because you can."

"Oh, please." I gave him a quick kiss, then grabbed his hand, pulling him towards the house. "You'd hold it over me as long as you could."

"I would totally fight you in Hell." He agreed with a laugh.

"What?" I laughed as we began climbing the porch stairs. "You still don't think we'd get into Heaven?"

Lucas turned at the top of the stairs to look out at the fire raging in Point Worth.

"I think we're too used to Hell to ever do well in Heaven, babe."

"Fair enough." I kissed him quickly again. "You ready?"

"Yeah." He nodded.

"*Are you two gonna suck face out there all day or are we gonna do this?*" Oma bellowed from somewhere inside the house. "*I'm too old to be waitin' around this long for anybody—even you two.*"

I rolled my eyes, and Lucas laughed, but hand in hand, we entered Oma's house, prepared for whatever awaited. No matter what that thing was, we were going to meet it together.

# Chapter 9

Oma was standing in the living room, hands on her hips, and though the lights were all out, I could see enough to know that she was alone. There was no one waiting with her, ready to jump out and attack Lucas and me as we entered the house. My first thought was to be a smart mouth and tell her to turn on a damn light so I could see all of her liver spots, but then I realized the lights might have been off for other reasons. With Point Worth on fire, Bloody Bones returning—and what was probably turning out to be the first stage of an apocalypse, lines were probably down all over town. Even if Oma wanted, the house might not have any power. For curiosity's sake, I reached over and flipped the switch on the wall. The darkness remained.

"I ain't standin' in the dark for my health," Oma said simply.

"Just checking," I replied.

"The power's out, genius."

"Got it."

"Rob." Lucas squeezed my hand. "Mrs. Wagner. Let's just stop fighting and being hateful. We're here so you can help us in any way that you can. But most of all, we need you to fix whatever you did to our memories. All of the fighting and insults are getting us nowhere."

"Fine." Oma threw her hands up in the air. "I guess I can keep from insulting smart mouth over here for a few minutes."

"Stop," I said.

Oma seemed to deflate, obviously unsure of what to do if she wasn't allowed to use her arsenal of hatred and insults.

"Well," Oma said, "I guess the best thing I can do is start with telling you about Bloody Bones. Well, reminding you, I guess."

"Why's that?" Lucas answered for us, causing me to glance over at him.

"Because that's where this all starts and ends." Oma waved him off. "Do the two of you remember the legend of Bloody Bones...or is that something your tiny little brains squeezed out when the genius over here made his wishes?"

"His wishes?" Lucas shook his head. "I don't really remember that."

"I don't either." I shrugged. "Not really. I mean...I remember that I made wishes...for some reason. But whatever you've done has made it hazy. I don't think I remember it for real."

"Well," Oma sighed, "old as I am, I don't know everything, but—"

"Imagine that," I mumbled.

Oma shot me a look, and Lucas gave me a disapproving, though amused look, but neither of them said anything.

"But," Oma glowered at me, "I know enough. Wish I had the book so I could tell it properly, but *someone* took it."

"The book?" Lucas perked up. "The book Rob had? It's in the car!"

Lucas started to move, as if to run for the car to retrieve the book, but Oma held a hand up.

"Why did you take the book?" She asked me. "I wanted to ask last night, but you was out of here like your ass was on fire."

"I thought it might help us get our memories back?" I shrugged as Lucas watched the two of us. "Maybe there was a spell or—"

"A spell!" Oma cackled. "That ain't no damn spellbook, you dumbass. That's the history of this damn land. It has the story of how Bloody Bones came to be. It's been passed down from villager to town folk, on and on, keeping the history of how this town came to be from generation to generation. For centuries—maybe longer—the elders would pass the story down to younger generations, reminding them of Bloody Bones and why we're here. They'd tell the story of The Oracle, The Guardian, and The Witch. Remind the younger generation that evil may sleep, but not for long. We must always be vigilant...in case he returns. And that asshole has popped up far too many damn times."

"What?" Lucas frowned.

"Yeah." Oma waved him off. "It's a storybook, really. But the story is real."

"I want to say that's all bullshit, but with what goes on in this town—this house—that just seems to be accurate. A storybook you kept hidden away under a damn bookcase for years. That checks out."

Oma just shrugged, agreeing with my assessment.

"Well," She continued, "once upon a time, as these stories always go, this land was filled with magic. People had barely even arrived, but they were thriving—best as people could in them days."

I glanced over at Lucas, and he just shrugged.

"No one knows why. No one knows how. No one even really remembers what might have caused it...but Bloody Bones used that magic to make himself corporeal. To give himself life. A body. What was he before? Hell if I know. Maybe he was a manifestation of people's bad thoughts, feelings, and intentions, but—"

"Big word for you," I mumbled.

Oma shot me a look.

"—***BUT***, he simply...came into being. Oh, at first, it was pretty harmless stuff. Grabbin' at the legs of people swimmin' in the lake. Mostly children. People started tellin' the story about '*Bloody Bones who lives in the lake and comes for bad children,*' thus, givin' this creature a name. Namin' somethin', givin' it recognition, gives it more power. Usin' his existence, givin' him a name, givin' him power over the minds of children, instillin' fear in someone with the knowledge of him—well, it just helped him become more powerful. He used the magic of this land to his advantage, makin' himself stronger. And, one day, he broke free from the power that held him to the land. A crack appeared one day. And it grew. And grew. From that crack, straight down to the pits of Hell, Bloody Bones rose."

"Again," I shrugged, "Ohio—portal to Hell—seems right."

Lucas hushed me, and Oma rolled her eyes.

"He began with simple mischief at first. Stealin' crops, saltin' fields so nothin' grew, fellin' trees, settin' fire to huts. Then he grew greedy. As time went on and the people who lived here got more and more advanced, he began feastin' on chickens and stealin' food, snatchin' the occasional child. And like idiots, those people told greater stories about Bloody Bones and disobedient children, addin' to his legend, makin' him more powerful."

Lucas was suddenly holding my hand tightly.

"Things probably would have went on like that for a much longer time...but suddenly, The Oracle and The Guardian appeared. The Guardian was born from this land, like Bloody Bones, with one mission, to seek out The Witch. The Oracle was the same—though her mission was to watch over this town, these lands, to sense whenever Bloody Bones was coming. So...The Oracle and The Guardian worked together...and they found The Witch. The first of her kind. Not much more than a child, The Guardian and The Oracle found that she possessed control over the magic of her people, a magic that was separate from Bloody Bones. A power he had not been able to pervert to his whims and wishes. For many months, they worked with The Witch, hidin' her away, instructing her on what needed doin'...and then, The Oracle and The Guardian watched as The Witch met Bloody Bones in battle.

"In the end...The Witch cast Bloody Bones down, trapping him in the lands once more. She was worse for the wear, but The Guardian and The Oracle knew they could nurse her back to health. But The Witch knew somethin' that they didn't. She knew that if she let them heal her, she would only be livin' to face Bloody Bones in battle again one day. So, she used the rest of the power that resided in herself to strengthen the seal that held Bloody Bones in the ground, protectin' her people for as long as possible."

"What happened to her?" I asked.

"Well, she died, 'course." Oma shrugged, though her eyes looked dewy. "She sacrificed herself to give her people even longer to be free of ole Red Eyes. But, as they watched The Witch die and sink into the ground, The Oracle and The Guardian knew they hadn't seen the last of Bloody Bones. Maybe it would take a hundred or more years for him to find his way out to fight again, but he wasn't gone for good. Just as that thought occurred to them, where The Witch had once laid, something peculiar sprouted from the ground."

"What was it?" Lucas whispered in rapt attention.

"A well." Oma turned her eyes to me.

"Well, well, well," I stated blandly.

"It would contain all of the magic of her family. There in case it was ever needed to defeat Bloody Bones again. Just in case the next witch needed some help. She not only sacrificed herself for her family—and the people of this land—The Witch cast them a lifeline should they ever need it."

"I see," I replied evenly, and I could feel Lucas' eyes on the side of my head.

"But your damn family," Oma pointed a finger in my face, "down through the centuries have been reckless and ignorant with that power. They've used it on whims and wishes. And here we are with Bloody Bones back—at his strongest—and you done fucked everything up."

"Yeah." I shrugged. "It's easy to blame the last person who made the same mistake dozens of people made before, Oma."

"Well," Oma waved me off, "they're all dead, so you have to take the cussin' for all of 'em, ya' damn idiot."

"Fair enough." I relented. "But how the fuck was I supposed to know?"

"Because I've told you this damn story at least a hundred goddamn times, that's how!"

"Well, in my defense, I don't remember."

Lucas was shifting from one foot to the other.

"And I told you!" She jabbed a finger at him next, making him jump. "But you two thought you was smarter than me—than The Witch who knew what she was doing when she left that well of magic for this family. She knew that one day Bloody Bones would come back so powerful that y'all would need that little extra somethin'. And everyone just squanders it. Fuckin' humans. You're all worthless half the damn time—and the other half of the time you're diggin' in your own asses about one thing or another that don't matter."

"That's all well and good, Oma." I snapped. "But where does that leave us? That didn't make me remember anything—well, maybe I have a few flashes of the past working around in my head right now, but nothing concrete. What good does any of this do us?"

"Now," Oma glared at me, "we're goin' down to the cellar."

"I'm not going into any goddamn cellar with you."

"Rob." Lucas squeezed my hand.

"Damn-fuckin-right you are," Oma growled. "We need somewhere safe so I can lift the damn veil from you two. So you can remember everything."

"The...the veil?" Lucas peeped.

Oma fluttered her fingers in the air.

"Yeah," She grumbled, "the damn spell I did to make you both dumber than usual. I'll reverse what I done did; you'll remember everything...then wise ass over here can decide what he's going to do!"

"What I'm going to do?" I frowned.

"About Bloody Bones, of course!"

"Why do I have to do anything? Why is that my job?"

"Because you're the last damn ancestor of The Witch." Oma barked. "This is your job. Like it or not, that's what you was born to do, Rob."

I started to say something hateful back but stopped myself.

"Ya' know what?" I snapped at her. "If I could sink into the ground and get away from you, I'd do it, you old bitch."

"Good!" She snapped back.

Lucas just held my hand.

"Now, let's get down in the damn cellar where we got some protection if anyone comes nosin' around here, and we'll do this damn thing."

Lucas and I looked at each other, our fingers twining together as we considered the request—well, *demand*—from Oma. My instincts told me that we should follow Oma into the cellar, let her do whatever magic she felt she had to do, and then face Bloody Bones when he showed up. However, something kept pinging around in my head, some little voice telling me there was a question that needed to be asked. Just as I was about to take a step towards Oma, pulling Lucas with me, I realized what the voice was saying.

"Wait," I said, causing Oma to halt in her tracks and turn to look at me. "You said everyone talking about Bloody Bones, telling his legend, adding to his myth, gave him more power?"

"Yeah?" Oma shrugged.

"People stopped talking about him." I shook my head. "I do remember that people in this town stopped talking about him. In fact, people stopped believing altogether. So...how is he more powerful now."

"Because he stopped relying on the whims of humans and found a new way to get magic." Oma waggled her head. "Every time he's come back—up until the last time—he was using the magic humans give all their Gods, and—"

"All their Gods?" Lucas asked.

"What's any deity but the creation of humans brought to life by myth?" Oma said simply. "Humans have a very peculiar magic of their own. They tell stories. Those stories spread from mouth to mouth until the story is the truth. Stories have power, Lucas Barkley. Just as humans give God power, they give Bloody Bones power."

"Oddly," I turned to Lucas, "that's pretty logical."

Lucas shrugged. When I turned back to Oma, she was smiling, happy with herself.

"Still don't like you any." I shrugged at her.

She frowned. "Well, when you idiots—*humans*—stopped talkin', stopped givin' him power...he started takin' it from the land. I suppose he didn't know he could do that before. But desperate times call for desperate measures. And he didn't just take it. He used it. Not just to rise up and try to come back, but to gain allies. This town's full of 'em, too."

"He's been giving families around here power?" I nodded slowly.

"Damn right, he has." Oma nodded firmly. "Nearly every damn family in this town is connected to the power he stole from the land. Whatcha think's gonna happen when he takes it back?"

"Shit." I sighed.

"Grandpa!" Lucas gasped.

"Ole Jackson's probably already met his maker." Oma waved him off casually.

"Oma!" I growled.

Lucas gasped again.

"Well," She said, "it's just the truth. Carlita, too. Maybe even Andrew."

Lucas was looking at me desperately, his eyes welling with tears.

"Well, I don't really care about Andrew, but—"

"Ya' should." Oma snorted. "He's been tryin' to help me make you leave this town again to make it safer. S'why he was a douchebag to ya'. Why he attacked you. He could control his damn wolf—don't be ridiculous. He did that because I asked it of him."

"Then why'd he ask me out on a second date?" I growled.

"Because he probably figured you'd put out?" Oma threw her hands up. "That's none my damn concern! And, right now, it shouldn't be yours, either. Are we goin' down in this damn cellar so I can give you two idiots back your memories, or are we gonna stand up here in the world's most boring circle jerk until he shows up to kill us all?"

Lucas was holding my one hand with both of his, tears silently trailing down his cheeks as he thought of his grandfather, Jackson Barkley, possibly being dead. I gave him the most understanding, warmest look I could muster, and he just nodded at me. I turned to face Oma once more.

"Lead the way you insensitive old hag."

"Fine." She snapped, turned on her heels, and stomped towards the kitchen.

Turning to Lucas, he just shook his head, letting me know that it was not the right time to try to comfort him. Nothing I could say would have made him feel better about what Oma had just said anyway. Instead of saying anything, or trying to hug or kiss him, I stepped towards the kitchen, dragging Lucas behind me. As we made our way into the kitchen, Lucas shuffling his feet, Oma was swinging the cellar door wide and heading down the steps. I stopped for a moment as I looked at the dark opening that led down below and swallowed hard. The best I could hope was that we got into the cellar, and Oma removed...*the veil*...she had placed on Lucas and me. Then I could fight Bloody Bones.

*What the actual fuck?*

That was the best hope I could imagine? Some crazy scheme that seemed like a fever dream?

As Lucas and I descended the stairs cautiously, ours heads whipping around, trying to watch our backs, fronts, and sides at all times, I knew that the best-case scenario in this situation was still a shitstorm. No matter how the pie was sliced, it was still going to be bad. Oma was standing in the middle of the cellar, where the well had once stood, her arms crossed over her chest, waiting on us when we stepped down onto the dirt floor of the cellar.

"You look like the Cowardly Lion and The Scarecrow off to see the Great and Powerful Oz. Where's Dorothy, ya' assholes?"

I ignored her.

"Carlita was The Oracle." It wasn't a question. "Like *The Oracle*—from your little story."

"Wasn't a *little story.*" She barked, her hands lowering to her sides.

"Whatever." I waved her off. "So…you're not my grandmother."

"I'm not." She said finally, her voice bland, as though she had to force herself to be emotionless.

"You're…The Guardian, I assume?"

She nodded. "Found the first witch, and I've been comin' back and dealin' with your dumbass family every time Carlita—*The Oracle*—sensed he was going to return."

Oma sighed, her eyes flashing to Lucas.

"Maybe," She stated wistfully, "if this night had any chance of turning out any other way than I know how it's gonna turn out, you could-a taken her spot, God rest her soul."

Lucas frowned as he chewed at his lip.

"Ya' got the gift." Oma shrugged. "Your foresight and all. I can kinda see her magics already trying to attach themselves to ya' now that their original vessel is gone."

"What?" Lucas whispered.

"If they had enough time, and I thought we'd make it through this night, I'd imagine I'd be helping a new oracle learn his craft. To help prepare us for the next battle."

"What does that mean?" I asked for Lucas.

"Your boyfriend has the gift." Oma waved a hand at him. "Came from the same magics that made me and Carlita. Now that Carlita's gone—*I know she's gone, I can't sense her anymore*—her magics will probably try to find a new oracle to inhabit. I imagine it would be Lucas. Ain't nobody else in this town got that kind of gift—or the wherewithal to use it as intended."

"So...Lucas would be your other half when this is all said and done?" I laughed bitterly. "And I'd just be the witch that gave his life so you could keep on watching Bloody Bones rise, and witches fall?"

"'Bout sums it up, yeah." Oma shrugged. "It's the way it's always been."

"I'm glad to see it pains you." I rolled my eyes.

Oma glared at me, though something in her eyes told me she wasn't mad. She was bitter.

"Just," Lucas interrupted before one of us could say something snarky to the other, "give us back our memories. Lift the veil...or whatever."

"Gladly." Oma nodded and stood up straight, squaring her shoulders.

Lucas and I kept our hands locked as Oma squared herself and planted her feet, her arms reaching out towards us, one hand pointed at Lucas, one at me. Then she smiled.

"This might sting a little." She chuckled.

Then there was a flash.

And a sting.

Oma didn't always lie about *everything.*

# Chapter 10

*"You will join us, goddamnit." Jason, barely decently covered in a pair of jeans, shoved a towel-clad Lucas into the locker. "It's your fate, you little asshole. I'm sick and tired of you giving me shit about it. This is who you're supposed to be."*

*Jason's forearm dug into Lucas' windpipe as Lucas' wet feet slipped and slid on the slick concrete floor of the locker room. The only thing keeping Lucas from falling and slipping all the way across the room and back into the shower—which he had just left—was Jason's forearm pinning him against the locker. If Jason pulled away suddenly, Lucas wasn't sure he could catch himself quickly enough to keep from busting his ass painfully on the floor. Or, maybe he would slide all the way across the room. Of course, the towel wrapped around his waist might have been enough to keep him from sliding too far.*

*Lucas had been so careful. Jason had been harassing him for months to join his pack, but Lucas had always been clever in avoiding Jason when he was alone. There was no way that Jason could fulfill his threats to turn Lucas into...*one of them...*if there were always witnesses to their exchanges. Even this night, only his third football game with the team, he had made sure he took an extra long shower. He waited until he was sure that all of the other guys had gotten showered, dressed, and left the locker room. The water in the showers had turned cold by the time Lucas finally twisted the knobs on the wall, and the water stopped cascading over his body. Shaking with* *cold, his fingers resembling prunes, Lucas had grabbed his towel, wrapped it around his waist, secured it, and headed to his locker to dress.*

*Of course, Jason was done being patient. He had been waiting for Lucas to emerge from the showers. At first, all Lucas could think was that he was grateful that Jason had not come into the showers after him. At least he had been patient enough to wait to have this exchange with him when they were both adequately covered up.*

*"I'm telling you, man." Jason laughed bitterly. "This isn't a choice. Eventually, we all gotta sign up."*

*"Sign up?" Lucas gasped, his hands clutching at Jason's forearm as he ground his teeth in pain.*

*"Bloody Bones, man." Jason grinned evilly, pushing his forearm harder into Lucas' throat.*

*Lucas' hands scratched at Jason's forearm, desperately trying to break free, or at least catch a breath of air.*

*"He's coming soon, man." Jason chuckled deeply. "And he needs us. You're either on his side…or you're against him."*

*"There are other ways." Lucas managed to gasp.*

*He didn't want to tell Jason what he felt in his gut, the things he just knew, but Lucas knew that Bloody Bones wasn't his only option. Somehow…he just knew it.*

*"Are you saying 'no'?" Jason growled, his jaw seemingly lengthening as Lucas struggled against the locker, his feet slipping and sliding on the floor.*

*Lucas' eyes bugged as Jason's forearm dug deeper into his throat, cutting off his oxygen. He watched through blurry eyes as Jason's jaw stretched, slight tufts of fur sprouting around what could only be described as a muzzle. Fang-like teeth slowly grew from Jason's mouth. The teeth of a wolf. Lucas struggled and slipped and slid as Jason's eyes turned red. Then his muzzle lowered to Lucas' arm.*

*Pain.*

*"Does it hurt?" Jackson Barkley asked as he knelt in front of Lucas, who was perched on the side of his bed rigidly. "Looks nasty."*

*"A little, I guess." Lucas' eyes were on the floor, by his grandfather's feet.*

*"That bruise 'round your neck is gonna be nasty." Lucas' grandfather sighed. "You gotta learned to stand up for yourself, Lukie."*

*Lucas looked up at his grandfather disdainfully.*

*"He's two years older, nearly a foot taller, and has fifty pounds on me, grandpa." Lucas snapped pitifully. "How am I supposed to stand up to him?"*

*Most people would expect a grandfather to bark back, to tell his grandson to 'be a man' or some other nonsense. Jackson Barkley was not that type of man—or grandfather.*

*"Lukie," Jackson reached out and laid a hand on Lucas' knee, "he's gonna see that you are immune. If you don't go changing into a wolf within a few moons, he's gonna know. That's all's I'm saying."*

*"I know." Lucas looked down.*

*Jackson rubbed Lucas' knee.*

*"He mentioned Bloody Bones," Lucas whispered.*

*"Don't say that name none," Jackson whispered back, but he was not cross with his grandson.*

*"I thought I had forgotten," Lucas said. "You told me to forget."*

*"I did."*

*"I remembered everything when he said that name." Lucas looked up into his father's eyes.*

*Jackson Barkley groaned and rose from his crouched position and sat down on the bed next to his grandson. He took Lucas' arm in hand and brought it closer to inspect.*

*"You'll just forget again," Jackson said.*

*"But maybe if I use—"*

*"No." Jackson snapped, and there was heat in his voice this time as he let Lucas' arm fall from his grip. "You forget everything you know again. Push it to the back of your mind. Never speak of it."*

*"But grandpa—"*

*"This conversation is over." Jackson Barkley stood from the bed abruptly and marched toward the door of Lucas' bedroom. "And another thing—"*

*Jackson turned to find Lucas looked down at his feet, his bitten arm cradled in his other.*

*"Aw, Christ." Jackson reached up to rub the back of his neck. "Look, Lukie..."*

*"What?"*

*"Your day is coming, son," Jackson stated lowly. "You aren't meant for what them powers was given to you for by...him. Your destiny is bigger than that. Better. Your destiny is good. I told*

*you what you'd be one day if you just wait. Be patient. Forget."*

*"Jason will just keep trying, Grandpa." Lucas looked up. "I believe you. I trust you. But Jason won't give up. What am I supposed to do?"*

*For the longest of moments, Jackson Barkley stared at his grandson. Finally, as if he had made up his mind about something, he straightened up in the doorway of the bedroom.*

*"Maybe you need a friend?" Jackson suggested. "Then you won't be alone and worrying all the time?"*

*"Everyone at school sucks." Lucas groaned and kicked at the floorboards with the toe of his shoe. "I mean, the people I'm supposed to hang with suck. The guys in football...well, ya' know. They're like Jason. The girls are dumb, and everyone else has their own thing going on. No one seems to want to really like me unless it's about being on the football team."*

*Jackson Barkley smiled.*

*"Well, most teenagers...suck, I suppose." He chuckled. "Maybe you need to find a friend who has different interests than yourself then?"*

*"Like who?" Lucas rolled his eyes but smiled. "Justin McCafferty? He picks his nose and eats it. We're in high school for crying out loud."*

*Jackson Barkley laughed.*

*"Well," Jackson said as his laughter tapered off, "I got a friend out there on the lake. Maybe you'd like her grandson? You go to school together, anyway."*

*"Who?" Lucas perked up, though he was cautious about any suggestions his grandfather might have about how to make friends.*

*"Bobby...nah, Robbie Wagner?"*

*Lucas felt his breath leave his lungs.*

*"Rob?" He whispered.*

*"If that's what he goes by, sure." Jackson shrugged and leaned against the doorjamb. "Esther Jean—his grandmother—was tellin' me that he gets lonely out there on the far edge of town out by the lake. Guess he ain't got a lot of kids—ahem, young men—who live out by him either. Maybe you could make friends with him?"*

*"He's," Lucas felt his cheeks warm at the thought of Rob Wagner, "kind of...weird."*

*Lucas didn't mean "weird." He meant to say something entirely different that would have led to a discussion he wasn't ready to have with his parents or grandfather yet.*

*"Well, weird's okay." Jackson shrugged with a grin. "As long as it ain't the booger picking kind, right?"*

*Lucas grinned and looked down at his shoes so that his rosy cheeks would be hidden by the shadows.*

*"Well," Mrs. Wagner stood at the kitchen counter as Rob and Lucas sat across from each other at the kitchen table, "ain't this a cute little playdate?"*

*Rob smiled at Lucas and turned his eyes to his grandmother.*

*"What?" Mrs. Wagner shrugged as Lucas sank into his chair, completely out of his element and with nothing to say.*

*"Oma." Rob shook his head in a playfully reprimanding way. "Go away."*

*"It's my house." She demanded, though there was no power in her words. "Fine. Fine. I'll go dust the fuckin' bookcases or somethin', I spose."*

*"Thank you." Rob chuckled nervously as his grandmother marched out of the room, pretending to be upset.*

*Lucas frowned, noticing that Mrs. Wagner hadn't bothered to find a feather duster or cloth with which to do her chores. Of course, he had always heard that Esther Jean Wagner was…odd…so he decided to not let it bother him any. Instead, he picked up the can of soda—or "sodey pop" as Mrs. Wagner had called it—and brought it to his lips. Rob mimicked his actions. The two boys sat in silence, only the sounds of effervescent bubbles in the cans as a soundtrack.*

*"So," Rob finally spoke, luckily before the silence had grown too thick, "you're on the football team, right?"*

*"Yeah," Lucas answered eagerly, glad to have something, anything, to talk about. "Uh, yeah. Um, I tried out. I'm a running back."*

*"Kind of cool for a freshman to be on the team." Rob smiled, trying to think of a way to direct the conversation.*

*"I mean," Lucas blushed slightly, "I guess. I'm just small and fast, so…"*

*"Easy for you to sneak the ball by other players?" Rob smiled.*

*"Yeah." Lucas agreed. "Season's over, though, so we're just stuck in practices now. Maybe I can actually get off the bench next year."*

*"I feel like I know you." Rob blurted out suddenly, then looked down. "I mean, obviously*

*that's stupid. We go to the same school, so of course, you'd seem, uh, familiar and stuff, right?"*

*"Right." Lucas' face was stuck between a smile and a frown. "But, I, uh, know what you mean. I feel like we've hung out before or something."*

*Rob shrugged.*

*"Did you go to CARNAVAL last year?" Rob asked. "I think I went to that. Around Halloween? It seems so long ago."*

*Rob gave a nervous chuckle as Lucas shrugged.*

*"I don't remember going," Lucas replied. "I mean…it was such a big deal, right? It seems like I was there. Everyone was talking about it, anyway. Maybe that's why?"*

*"Yeah." Rob agreed. "Maybe."*

*The two boys took sips of their sodas again, looking anywhere but at each other. Suddenly, Rob got a curious grin on his face, then leaned in conspiratorially.*

*"It's like I can remember the taste of the popcorn and cotton candy."*

*Lucas smiled. "Right? All popcorn and cotton candy from carnivals tastes the same, though, right?"*

*"Yeah." Rob relented. "Wish I had gone. People wouldn't shut up about that for forever."*

*Lucas laughed at the way Rob rolled his eyes and sunk down in his chair as though he had been through war.*

*"CARNAVAL this, CARNAVAL that." Rob groaned comically. "I bet no one's parents let 'em go anyway. And it was gone the next day, so…"*

*"Right?" Lucas laughed. "I mean, Jason and—the guys on the team—they all probably went. I heard them talking about it a lot. But…"*

*"What?" Rob leaned in, grinning. "What were you going to say?"*

*"Nothing." Lucas shook his head with a smile.*

*"Nah." Rob shook his head with an impish grin. "You can't leave me hanging like that. You started a sentence; you have to finish it."*

*"Is that how that works?" Lucas laughed.*

*"Yep." Rob nodded as he grabbed his soda. "House rules."*

*"Fine." Lucas rolled his eyes, though he was amused. "Jason and the other guys on the team are kind of liars. That's all. They probably didn't go either. Just them wanting to be cool and stuff."*

*Rob grinned widely.*

*"I don't really tell anybody anything worth hearing." He said. "So, they'll never find out what you think of them."*

*"Promise?"*

*"Promise." Rob made a cross over his heart with a fingertip. "Not a word to a single person."*

*"Cool." Lucas grabbed his soda.*

*Rob leaned in his chair so that he could look through the kitchen door to the other part of the house where, presumably, Mrs. Wagner was dusting.*

*"Do you want to see something cool?" Rob asked. "A secret of mine?"*

*Lucas chewed at his lip.*

*He wanted Rob to tell him or show him anything he wanted.*

*And he would take any secret to his grave if he had to.*

*"Yeah, man." Lucas nodded slowly.*

*"Come on." Rob stood from the table, grabbing his soda as he whispered. "I want you to meet Ernst."*

*"Ernst?" Lucas frowned as he followed Rob's lead.*

*"Shhh." Rob held a finger to his lips. "It's a secret, remember?"*

*Lucas laughed nervously, then turned his voice to a whisper. "Okay."*

*"Up in my room." Rob jerked his head towards the other part of the house. "But you can't tell anyone. Promise?"*

*"Promise."*

*"Like, for real." Rob turned to Lucas, still grinning, though he looked unsure.*

*Lucas' eyes met Rob's. Another flash of lightning in his gut.*

*And Lucas suddenly knew something else.*

*He knew why he had told Jason there were other ways besides Bloody Bones.*

*"Promise." Lucas breathed out.*

*Rob smiled. "Come on."*

*He winked and exited the kitchen. Lucas followed right at his heels.*

# Chapter 11

*My mother was sprawled on the kitchen floor, the cast iron skillet, and the pancakes it once held on the stove was at her feet. Her eyes were wide open, and her mouth hung slack—she saw nothing and had no more words to say. Standing there, my small fists clenched at my sides, tears streaming down my face, I waited for my father to return. When the man in the dark hood had burst through the kitchen door and...did...what he did...to my mother...my dad had not been close behind him. Flashes of light had filled the kitchen and what I could only call "war screams" poured from my father's mouth as he...fought?...with the man who had hurt my mother.*

*As I waited for my father, I shuffled tentatively towards my mother, wondering if I should try to wake her up. Why wouldn't she get up off of the floor instead of lying there next to the ruined breakfast? Dad had chased off the scary man with the dark hood, so there was no reason for my mother not to move now. When I got close to my mother, I jerkily reached down, my hand slowly uncurling, reaching for her arm.*

*"Muh-mommy?" I had whispered.*

*My hand had barely had time to connect with her cooling flesh before my father had come soaring through the backdoor once again. Fury was painted his face. Until his eyes landed on mine, and he saw me touching my mother's arm. He came to me swiftly and scooped me up, burying my face in his chest, holding me to him. I didn't know how to ask him...was my mom dead?*

*What happened to my mom between the moment I touched her arm, and my dad put me to bed, I didn't know. We never went back into the kitchen. Dad and I spent the day in the house, refusing to turn on lights, even after the sun went down. He held me in his lap, his arms wrapped around me, not letting go unless I needed to eat or use the bathroom. Dad stayed by my side all day long, whispering to me how much he loved me, telling me stories about my birth, the first years of my life, what I meant to him and my mother. How I would be okay, and he would never let anyone harm me. His lips pressed against my forehead and top of my head more times than I could count in those hours between breakfast and bedtime.*

*Finally, when the moon was high in the sky, Dad took me upstairs and changed me into my pajamas. Then he tucked me into bed snuggly, the odd smile on his face illuminated by the sliver of moonlight that peeked through the blinds in my room. He whispered to me that he had to "take care of something," but if he wasn't able to come back, I would have someone to take care of me instead. Someone who would protect me just as fiercely as he and my mother had. So, no matter what, I shouldn't miss him if he didn't return. I was still too confused over what had happened to my mother and what he was telling me to really understand.*

*But he sat on the side of my bed, stroking my hair and back until I drifted off to sleep. I don't know when I fell asleep, or when Dad left my bedside, but when I woke the next morning, bright morning light was peeking through the blinds, and my dad was gone.*

*Knock.*

*Knock.*

*KnockKnockKnock.*

*Wearily, rubbing at my eyes, I stumbled down the steps into the living room, wondering why Dad or Mom hadn't answered the door. Why was someone allowed to knock so loudly and so much so early in the morning? A flash of my mom lying on the kitchen floor burst through my mind, and I frowned, trying to think of what that meant. As I stood at the base of the steps, the knocking still sounding, I remembered Dad saying that he had something to take care of, so I might have someone to watch over me for a while. Hesitantly, I shuffled over to the front door and grabbed the knob with both of my small hands. I swung the door wide, squinting at the bright early morning light as it burst through the door.*

*"Well," I heard a woman's voice, her figure haloed by the sun, "you're a lot smaller than I'm used to, that's for sure."*

*Slowly, my eyes adjusted, and I was able to open them a little wider to see who was speaking to me. A woman I had never seen before, maybe a little shorter than my mom was, gray hair, wrinkled face, stern expression, yet eyes that twinkled—imposing for a five-year-old—stood before me, arms folded over her chest. A large suitcase on wheels was sitting on the porch upright next to her, its handle extended, as though she had just dragged it up the steps.*

*"Who are you?" I had asked, my bottom lip jutting out in what I had hoped was a brave and defiant manner.*

*I was a man. This was my house. All five-year-old boys think that.*

*"I'm Esther Jean Wagner." The woman looked down at me sternly, though the warmth in her eyes was apparent. "You can call me Oma."*

*"What's an Oma?" My nose crinkled up.*

*"Grandmother." She waggled her head. "I'm your dad's mother."*

*Without further explanation, she grabbed the handle of her bag and swung it over the threshold into the house. I backed up quickly to avoid getting knocked over by the movement. The lady…Oma?…followed the bag, looking around the house. Once she was inside, she folded her arms over her chest once more and looked around, taking in her surroundings as her bag stood next to her once again. For a beat, I just stared at her back, wondering who this woman was who claimed to be my grandmother. Then, she turned her head and glanced over her shoulder at me. Our eyes met.*

*Oma.*

*Of course.*

*Dad's mom.*

*My grandmother.*

*"I've never met you before," I stated stupidly as I gently pushed the door shut, chewing at my lip.*

*"I've been gone for a spell, Robbie," Oma said. "But your dad said he had to take care of some things, so he needed me to look after you."*

*"Oh."*

*"I'm not as mean as I look." She winked down at me as I rounded her imposing figure. "Usually."*

*"You look pretty mean," I admitted though I wasn't sure if that was the right thing to say.*

*"I have my moments." She shrugged sharply. "But you don't give me no sass, and I won't sass back. That sound like a fair deal?"*

*Thinking about this, I slowly started to nod as I chewed at my lip.*

*"Good." She finally smiled down at me, her arms falling to her sides. "Have ya' had breakfast, Robbie?"*

*"No." I shook my head. "I just woke up and my mom...my mom..."*

*She waved me off, smiling, though her eyes were sad.*

*"Don't worry about all that." She said brightly. "Oma's here now. And I brought some friends."*

*"Friends?" I asked, my lip chewing intensifying.*

*"Wanna see what's in my suitcase?" She asked, a mischievous grin coming to her face as she bent down slightly.*

*"I don't know."*

*She stood up sharply, her nose hooking into the air haughtily, though she looked down at me through the corner of her eye. That twinkle never went away.*

*"Well, maybe I don't want to show you then." She waggled her head.*

*I couldn't help it. I giggled. She held her haughty pose a moment longer, then turned her head down to smile at me.*

*"It ain't nothin' that will bite ya' none." She said reassuringly. "Just some little helpers while your dad is gone."*

*"Okay." I was nodding slowly again.*

*"So," She asked once more, "you wanna see?"*

*"Okay." I agreed hesitantly. "You're not going to scare me, are you?"*

*"Not on purpose."*

*I shrugged. "Okay."*

*Oma smiled warmly and turned to her suitcase, bending over to reach for the zipper. I watched with fascination—and a bit of fear—as she pulled the zipper three-quarters of the way around the suitcase, slowly pulling back the flap. At first, nothing happened, but then, ever so slowly, a small humanoid hand peeked out. I gasped, and the hand froze. My eyes shot up to Oma, and she just winked at me. My eyes went back to the bag, and I watched as a hand became an arm, then a torso and head…and a small human-like…thing…stepped out of the suitcase. It was even shorter than me, wringing its hands and looking around, as though unsure of its surroundings. I gasped again as another creature stepped out of the bag, then another…eventually five of these…things…stood in the living room with Oma and me.*

*"How did they all fit in there?" I looked up at Oma with saucer-like eyes.*

*"Magic, of course." She winked.*

*My eyes met Oma's, and something passed between us.*

*I grinned.*

*"Goddamnit, Robbie." Oma cursed as she rolled her eyes. "Ya' gotta stop doin' that."*

*"Sorry." My cheeks were warm as I winced down at the char marks on the tablecloth.*

*"How many times have I told you that you have to control yourself?" She barked, though her heart wasn't in it. "If you keep doin' that, people are going to know about you."*

*"Sorry," I repeated.*

*Ernst scuttled under the table and stood up next to my chair, his hand reaching for mine. I did my best to smile at him as he gave me a reassuring look. Oma was snatching the cloth off of the table, yet another blunder of mine that caused damage to something in the house. Ever since she had been trying to teach me how to tap into my magic and control it, all I'd done was mess things up. It was a lot for an eight-year-old to figure out as quickly as she wanted me to do. Magic didn't like to have people telling it what to do. Sometimes it did whatever the hell it wanted.*

*"And you." Oma's eyes shot over to land on Ernst, causing both Ernst and me to wince and shrink back, though he refused to let go of my hand. "You ain't doin' him no favors treatin' him like a baby."*

*"Ain't mean nuffin' by it, Missus." Ernst managed. "He's jus' a boy."*

*"Just a boy?" Oma rolled her eyes and wadded up the tablecloth. "The two of you are a pair, aren'tcha?"*

*Oma gave us both once last withering look before she stood from the table, the bundled-up tablecloth in her arms, and then she marched out the back door. Obviously, she was going to pitch the ruined cloth in the outside garbage so that no one would ever see it and ask questions. Not that we had many visitors—and even if we did, they wouldn't be going through our garbage, inside or out. I looked down at Ernst, disgusted with myself as he gave my hand a squeeze.*

*"It's a'ight, Rob." He reassured me, his other small hand coming up to pat the top of my hand while his other held it. "You'll ge' the hang o' it."*

*"I'm awful." I groaned. "I don't even know why this matters. I mean...I'm going to end up dead anyway, right?"*

*Ernst's face turned up, and he thumped my hand.*

*"Now, don' go talkin' like all tha'." He gave me a stern look. "Ya' gonna end up 'owever you wan' to end up. And ya' will get the 'ang of this."*

*"Maybe." I sighed. "Thanks for...being my friend, Ernst."*

*Ernst's little cheeks turned pink.*

*"What?" I asked, finally smiling at him.*

*"Never 'ad no friend before." He mumbled. "'Specially with your kind. Nah supposed ta anyway."*

*"Well," I shrugged, a trait I had learned from Oma over the previous years, "I keep breaking every other rule she gives me. We can break that one, too."*

*Ernst grinned impishly up at me as we squeezed each other's hands.*

*"I'm honored ta be yer frien', Rob."*

*"Forever, Ernst." I nodded and leaned down to hug him. "Forever."*

Like stepping out of a fog, things changed. I was no longer remembering my life as a series of memories or dreams, drifting overhead incorporeally, looking down at the events, but instead stepping up to a stage to watch them be acted out. It was almost like I was walking up to the front row of a theater and taking my seat, waiting for the show to start, but I was the only one with a ticket. I gazed out at the scenery before me as nothingness dissolved and was replaced with vague shapes and blurs, slowly coming into focus.

The play...*maybe movie?*...started with a view of a field of lush, green grass, and I immediately knew that I was looking at the land where Oma's—*my family home*—should have been. Except there was no house. But there were more trees. The grass looked more...*wild.* What would once be called Lake Erie was off in the distance. A young girl skipped into frame, but lazily, as if in slow motion. I stared up at the scene as I—*sat there, I guess?*—and watched the young girl, probably no more than ten-years-old enter the frame of my vision. In the middle of the field, the girl fell to her knees gleefully, then laid back in the grass, staring up at the brilliantly blue, sunny sky overhead.

Lying there in the grass, the girl's eyes closed, and she smiled, beatific in her innocence and happiness. I couldn't help but smile, though in the back of my mind, I remembered why I was experiencing these things. For several moments, I watched the girl in the grass, eyes closed, smiling at nothing...and everything...and then two people stepped into frame. Oma and Carlita. From the girl's garb and the clothing of the two people I knew already, I ascertained that this had happened so long ago that I had no way of putting a specific date to the events.

Carlita was the first to open her mouth, which startled the girl, though I couldn't hear what Carlita said, nor could I hear the girl shriek as she sat up quickly and scurried backward like a crab several feet. Oma stepped forward, her hands out as though to calm the girl, speaking mutely as the girl looked up at the two of them warily. For what seemed like forever, but was probably only seconds, I watched the three of them interact silently, not even one piano chord played to this silent movie, and then the girl rose to her feet. She took Oma's hand with a smile, which Oma returned, and then they walked away, my vision going black.

All I could hear was my heart in my chest, thuh-thumping for the space of a few breaths before the blackness started to fade away, revealing the same field once again, only at night this time. I gasped, though I couldn't hear that either, as Bloody Bones stood there in his black hooded cloak, fire shooting forth from an upraised hand at the girl. Oma and Carlita were standing several yards away, near the woods, watching as the girl returned her own magics in Bloody Bones direction. I watched in horror, seeing the toll this display was taking on the child, not much older than she had been in the first scene.

The fight wore on for several minutes, back and forth between Bloody Bones and the girl, but finally, with what I could only assume was a scream of rage, Bloody Bones was defeated. He reached towards the sky with fury and panic as the ground split open and he was pulled beneath, scratching and clawing, screaming silently at the girl. Once Bloody Bones had been sealed away, the ground swallowing him and sealing after him, the girl fell to her knees, exhausted and bleeding. Carlita and Oma stepped away from the woods, relieved smiles on their faces, as though they would approach the girl.

Disdainfully, the girl turned her head to glare at the two, making them stop in their tracks, suddenly afraid of this progeny of theirs. With a mouth twisted up in a howl, magic seemed to burst from the girl, spilling out and over the land, sliding over everything in its path. Without hearing a sound, or any narration, I knew this girl was imbuing the land with her magic, sealing Bloody Bones away for as long as the magic could hold. I gasped, though still soundlessly, as the girl fell to the Earth. In direct contrast to how it had accepted Bloody Bones, the Earth accepted the girl, cradling her like a baby in a bassinet, as if lulling her to sleep, slowly absorbing her into the ground, then sealing shut behind her. Magic continued to glimmer, even as the ground sealed gently shut around her body, sparkling over the surface of the land, the trees, the lake in the distance.

Seconds ticked by as Carlita and Oma stared at where the girl had been, until suddenly, a well slowly sprouted from the ground, growing inch by inch until it was waist-high to a man and as wide as a human is tall. Oma and Carlita stared at this strange artifact, unsure of what to make of it. But when green light began emanating from its depths, bathing the ground around it in a sickly green halo, Oma and Carlita looked at each other with concern.

These scenes played over and over in front of me, fading to black, reappearing, disappearing, Bloody Bones fighting to his death. But always with a different opponent. Sometimes a young girl. Sometimes a boy. Sometimes a teenage boy or girl. The well stood watch as they met on this field. Then, after several versions of this fight, a house was the backdrop to the fight, with no well in sight, obviously tucked away in its cellar.

In between each fight, flashing scenes of people peering into the well, their faces illuminated by a sickly green glow, greedy smiles on their faces showed before my eyes. A fight, a different person staring into the well. A fight, a new person going to seek the magic in the well. Over and over, again and again, time passing as battles were fought, and people became greedier and more envious.

Finally, when the scene faded to black, then slowly faded back to show another fight, and I saw a moonlit night, with my father stepping into frame, I screamed.

And I finally heard sound.

*"What is it?" I heard my voice.*

*Looking around, all I could see was darkness. But I had heard my own voice...well, my younger voice...so I knew that I should be seeing something in this vision.*

*"The source of your family's magic."*

*That was Oma's voice.*

*Slowly before me, like when the vision had started previously, a scene came into view. Barely breaking through the darkness at first, then gradually getting lighter and brighter until I could see what was going on. Oma and I were in the cellar of the house. I was on one side of the well, and she was on the other. Clearly, I remembered the day I had wandered into the cellar—maybe thirteen-years-old—and found the strange structure right in the center of the room. Oma had always told me not to go in the cellar, going out of her way to remind me that I should never go down those stairs. One day, curiosity got the better of me. Though, when I had finally gone against her wishes and Oma had found me, my eyes had been on the well. I had never looked up at her when we spoke in the dank and dark room, instead looking into the depths of the well. Watching this scene replay, from the outside looking in, I was able to watch Oma instead of the well.*

*She was smiling.*

*Smirking.*

*Plotting. She had been plotting.*

*Of course, she had wanted me to go into the cellar eventually. That's why she had kept bringing it up for those many years. Now she had gotten me where she wanted me.*

*"Is it always here?" My younger self whispered.*

*She shrugged, only acting with part of her body. The smile never left her face as I stared down into the well.*

*"It comes and goes." She said, staring down at my younger self leaning over the edge of the well. "Shows itself when it wants to or needs to."*

*"Why's it here?"*

*"I done told you." She said. "It's the source of all your family's magic. It's here for you if you ever need it. Unfortunately, some of your kinfolk have been dippin' into it over the years and—"*

*"Dipping into it?"*

*She made a crude sound but never stopped smiling. Oma had gotten me exactly where she had needed me to begin moving the pieces on the chessboard.*

*"Yeah." She stated flippantly. "Idiots used some of the magic. Thinkin' it could give them money or power or some other nonsense that they wanted. They used it for wishes."*

*"Wishes?" My younger self breathed the word, fascinated.*

*"Wishes." Oma reiterated. "Thought the well could solve their problems instead of handlin' the problems themselves. But wishes are only as good as the person making 'em. Bunch of idiots. Now, we need to get out of here."*

*"Would it grant me a wish?" I had asked dreamily, staring down into the dark depths of the well.*

*There it was. Looking at this scene from the outside, I saw the grin on Oma's face widen. That's what she had wanted me to know—she wanted that thought in my head, chewing away at all of my other thoughts for as long as it could.*

*"I suppose." She said, then suddenly the grin was gone. "Now, get off that damn well. We're*

*going back upstairs, and I never want you to come down here again. Don't even think about it. Don't talk about it to no one."*

*"Oma." My younger self pushed back from the well and looked up at her, my bottom lip jutting out.*

*"Don't 'Oma' me, mister." She jabbed a finger at the stairs. "I ain't got many rules around here, but this one I mean."*

*"Fine." My younger self rolled his eyes and started marching towards the stairs.*

*As my younger self disappeared out of frame, Oma's eyes followed him. When he was gone, Oma took one last look at the well, the grin returning to her face. She laid a hand on the edge of the well, giving it a soft pat as she smiled down at it, then she too was heading for the stairs.*

*'Everything Little Thing She Does Is Magic' by The Police was playing on the little radio on the kitchen counter when I walked into the room. Bright summer sunlight was pouring through the windows in the house, making everything look white and golden and nearly celestial. All of the curtains and drapes had been pushed back on their rods to help welcome the first day of summer. The house was sparkling clean and smelled of Oma's favorite lavender cleaner. I staggered down the stairs, all wonky elbows and joints, my hair surely sticking up in spikes all over my head, rubbing my fists into my eyes. My bare feet*

*padded down the stairs and then across the floor of the living room towards the kitchen. It was my last summer before I started Big Boy School. Talks had been given to me over and over again about what to expect, the friends I'd make, the teachers I would love, the things I would learn. All I cared about that summer morning was getting some of the food in the kitchen that was scenting the house from top to bottom: bacon and eggs and butter and maple-y goodness.*

*When I entered the kitchen, I immediately saw her standing there, back turned to me, poking around in a skillet on top of the stove. My eyes lit up as an evil grin came to my face, and I tiptoed across the linoleum floor in the kitchen, sneaking up on her. I grabbed ahold of her sides, my head barely coming up past her butt, making her scream out in feigned shock. She had heard me walking up behind her, but it didn't matter. She let my five-year-old self pretend that I had snuck up and startled the daylights out of her. She spun around, hand to chest, gasping as she looked down at me with wide eyes. Then her face broke into a smile, and she dropped to kneel before me. Her arms went around me immediately as she smothered my face with kisses.*

*"Good morning, Robbie!" My mother managed to get out between my squealing and squirming as she smothered me with her kisses. "Good morning, my little ray of sunshine!"*

*"Mommy!" I squealed, pretending that I wanted to get away, but I was really wanting my mother's kisses to keep going until I was exhausted and collapsed in her arms.*

*I wanted to feel my mom's arms around me, comforting and loving me, leading me to the table for my breakfast. The smothering kisses and squeezing arms lasted for what was a very long time, but not to a five-year-old. Finally, my mom pulled back, her hands going to my shoulders so that she could get a good look at me. Immediately, one hand went to my head, to try and pat down the multitude of cow-licks in my hair. She smiled to herself as she gave up after a few seconds. My hair never wanted to do what she wanted it to do, and that was a battle she was slowly losing. Her hand went to my chin, pinching it between her fingers as she winked at me.*

*"Did you leave your appetite in bed, or is it here with you?"*

*I giggled. So silly.*

*"I'm so hungry, mommy!"*

*"What do you want for breakfast, baby?"*

*"What did you make?"*

*"What do you want?"*

*I giggled. This was our game.*

*"What did you make, mommy?"*

*She smiled widely.*

*"What do you want?"*

*"I want eggs and bacon and pancakes!" I crowed towards the ceiling, excited for a new day, full of endless possibilities and wonder.*

*The way a five-year-old lives each day...with possibility.*

*"Well," Mom kissed my forehead quickly, "you must have read my mind. That's exactly what I made."*

*Cheering, I headed over to the table, my mom patting me on the butt as I turned away from her. I sat down, yawning and rubbing my eyes again as my mom got a plate from the cabinet in Oma's kitchen and went over to the stove to serve my breakfast. That was probably the best thing about being so young—no real responsibility, all the wonders of the world, and your mom served you breakfast. As I sat there, listening to the spatula scrape against the cast iron skillet, I couldn't help but wonder where Oma and my father were. They always had breakfast with us in the morning. In fact, Oma was usually the first person down in the kitchen. She usually made our breakfast. Sometimes mom did...but not very often. Frowning to myself, I rubbed my eyes with my balled-up hands again, trying to chase the last of the sleep away.*

*Just as I was turning in my seat to peek at my mother over the chair back, I felt it. The rumbling in the floor. At first, it just felt like a train passing nearby, though there were absolutely no train tracks anywhere near Oma's house. My eyes grew wide as the rumbling turned into shaking, and the whole house seemed to shake with the movement. A low roar began, then louder and louder until it sounded like a tornado was about to rip the house apart. I looked at my mother in terror as she turned to me, the half-filled plate in her hand, her own eyes wide with concern. No...with absolute terror.*

*"Mommy?" I squealed as loudly as I could over the sound.*

*"Stay there, Robbie!" My mom replied desperately, her hand unsteady as she reached out to set the plate on the kitchen counter as the house shook.*

*The plate clattered to the floor, shattering, food flying everywhere as I grabbed onto the chair, trying not to fall off of my seat. Next, it was the small radio falling off of the kitchen counter, its crash to the floor muted by the roaring and shaking. The roaring and shaking increased until I knew that I would fall from my seat to the hard ground below. My mother held onto the kitchen counter, trying to stay on her feet and also not step on the broken plate shards or chunks of greasy food. Suddenly, as though it had never even started, the roaring and the shaking stopped. We were left in Oma's deathly quiet kitchen, me holding onto my chair, terrified, and my mother gripping the kitchen counter as though her life depended upon it. Slowly, she turned to look at me, her face ashen, concern etched all over it.*

*"Muh-mommy?" I peeped.*

*My mother's mouth moved, but whatever came out was muffled, as though she were speaking underwater.*

*Then the roaring and shaking were back, and green light filled the room.*

*"Robbie!" My mother screeched as someone in a black hooded cloak flew through the backdoor.*

Oma had fucked with the only memory I had of my mother. But she hadn't done enough to make me completely forget it. She hadn't overlooked trying to inject herself into the memories I had before she appeared...she just hadn't done a good job. She wasn't as powerful as she thought.

*Are you scared?*

*No. I'm just lost.*

*I'd be scared.*

*I have no reason to be scared. I just don't know what to do. Things are changing. She's worried.*

*What do you think we should do?*

*I don't know. I don't know anything right now.*

*I wish I could help you.*

*We could…run away.*

*Together?*

*Would you run away with me?*

*Of course, I…did you see that?*

*What?*

*Rob! Run!*

*Why? What did you see?*

*Rob!*

*"Were you waiting for me?"*

*Lucas was standing at the bottom of the bleachers, his letterman jacket on, making him look as sexy as he was. I was sitting in the bleachers, my boring coat pulled tightly around my torso to keep me warm. I had been waiting on Lucas. Just like I always did.*

*"Of course, I was waiting on you," I replied, my voice not as deep as it now was. "I'm always waiting for you."*

*He smiled.*

*"I thought I was always waiting for you."*

*"Well," I shrugged comically, "one of us is always waiting. But...the wait is always worth it, right?"*

*"Abso-fucking-lutely," He replied. "Don't you get scared out here all alone? What if someone tried to get you?"*

*"You'd protect me."*

*"How can you be so sure?"*

*I shrugged. "I just know."*

*"I'd argue," He said, "but I'd be wrong. And I don't like being wrong."*

*"You nearly fumbled the last pass."*

*"I held on. For you."*

*"For me?" I chuckled.*

*"So we'd have a reason to celebrate."*

*"How do you think we should celebrate?"*

*"Maybe you can give me one of your amazing kisses?" He said, glancing around, as though he thought we might not be alone.*

*"You're the football star," I said as I lifted my legs to place my feet on the bleacher row below me. "Show me your skills. Come get it. Make a play."*

*Lucas grinned wickedly then slowly stalked up the stairs, his eyes never leaving mine. When he got to my row, he stepped over my leg, then brought his other leg over it as well, positioning himself between my legs. He looked down at me as his hand came up to cup the side of my face as I looked up at him. I wanted him to kiss me so badly.*

*"You're...beautiful."*

*I couldn't help but laugh. "Is that a compliment for a guy?"*

*"I wasn't talking about your looks."*

*That made me swallow back any retort.*

*"Do you want me to kiss you again?"*

*"Yes." I exhaled.*

*"Do you love me?" He asked.*

*"Yes." I breathed the word. "I love you."*

*Lucas sighed.*

*"I love you, too."*

*Then he leaned down, and his lips found mine. For several long seconds, our lips, no longer amateurish in their movements, pressed together passionately. When Lucas finally pulled away, he was smiling, his eyes dreamy, but there was also concern.*

*"Is tonight the night?" He asked gently, his fingers finding my hair.*

*"Yes." I nodded slowly, my eyes closing at the feel of his fingers in my hair.*

*"Are we still going to...ya' know?" He whispered his question.*

*"Yes." I tried to smile, but I was nervous. Not for the sex, but for the second part of our plan. "And then..."*

*"I don't want you to go." He swallowed hard, fighting his tears back.*

*"I don't want to go," I said. "But...I have to. You know that, right?"*

*"I wish I could go with you."*

*"Me, too."*

*"But you'll come back."*

*"Always."*

*"We'll always be together?"*

*"Even in death."*

*Oma was in the kitchen like she always was, preparing another breakfast, humming a tune to herself, cupboards suddenly slamming shut, and shadows shifting as I gamboled into the room. Bacon and biscuits and sausage gravy perfumed the air—the signature scent of Oma's house in the morning. Too hungry to entertain propriety, I plopped down into one of the kitchen chairs, prepared to eat. I was hungry. I was always hungry.*

*"What have I told you about flingin' your ass into my kitchen chairs?" Oma turned around; the large kitchen spoon in her hand was coated with gravy.*

*It made my mouth water.*

*"I'm sorry, Oma." I blushed. "Your cooking just always smells so good."*

*"I guess I can take that as an apology."*

*She cackled and turned back to the stove. Oma had rules in her house and a strict sense of what was and wasn't proper behavior. While she was quick to correct breaking the rules or displaying improper behavior, she was just as ready to laugh and forgive. Oma wasn't one to ever genuinely hold a grudge against anyone. Besides the Kelly family. As far as I knew, she'd never actually punished me for anything. Of course, Oma had a way with her looks and her words that let one know you would never want to suffer one of her punishments. So...I was a pretty good kid.*

*"Now," Oma said, the metal spoon scratching against the cast iron skillet, "what have you been up to the last few days?"*

*Summer sun was streaming through the window, making everything look soft and lazy and warm.*

*"Nothing." I shrugged.*

*"Nothin'." She snorted. "Nothin' my wrinkled ass, Robbie."*

*"Oma..."*

*She waggled her head. "Rob."*

*"Thank you." My pubescent voice cracked.*

*"I'll never get used to calling you that." She turned to me, putting her fists against her hips. "You're not a 'Rob.' You're too damn sweet to go by 'Rob.' I'm just goin' to call you 'Robbie' until you feel like a 'Rob,' and you can hate me if you want."*

*She gave me a wink and turned back to the stove. Since Oma's back was turned and she couldn't see it, I let myself smile.*

*"You've been stayin' away from the house from sun up to sun down the last few days." Oma teased over her shoulder. "To me, that spells out that you're sweet on some girl."*

*I shrugged, though Oma couldn't see it, as I sat at the table.*

*"You just gon' be quiet about it?" Oma chuckled to herself. "Ain't nothin' wrong with a fifteen-year-old boy catchin' sweet on a girl. All y'all go through it. Bunch of hormonal idiots just waiting for a chance to smooch...and do other things...with some willing girl."*

*My cheeks were red, and I was staring down at the table. Oma talking to me about the birds and the bees—such as it was—was bad enough. The fact that I didn't have a thing for any of the girls at school was another. Oma turned to me, her eyes locking onto mine.*

*"You're going to be a heartbreaker, Robbie," She sighed. "I mean, hell...just look atcha. Now that you're growing into yourself. You make sure you're bein' a gentleman until they tell you it's okay to act otherwise. Don't you let me hear a single word about you treatin' a girl wrong."*

*"You won't, Oma," I mumbled.*

*"Good."*

*She turned back to the stove.*

*"I don't have any crushes on any girls anyway." I found myself practically whispering.*

*"Well, that's okay, too." Oma nodded to herself. "Ain't nothin' wrong with bein' a late bloomer. Or never bloomin' at all. Keep you out of trouble as long as we can."*

*Oma laughed. I didn't.*

*There's a time in every young person's life where they decide the person they want to be with their parents—or their parental figure. Do they want to show their most authentic self and risk that it won't be good enough...or do they try on a persona so that they don't have to find out if the person they truly are is good enough to be loved? My teenage self chose the former.*

*"There's a boy I like, though." I felt the truth slide from my mouth.*

*The "skritch-skritch" of the spoon in the skillet stopped, and Oma seemed to freeze at the stove. My teenage heart palpitated within my chest as I waited for whatever was to come to...come. Thick, heavy silence grew between us in the kitchen as bacon sizzled in the other skillet, creating a soundtrack comprised of delicious sounds and smells. Just when I thought that I might scream out just to break the tension, the "skritch-skritch" of the spoon in the skillet started up again. Oma let the spoon rest against the side of the skillet and turned to me again, her hands on her hips once more.*

*"You know they got one them 'LGBT' centers over in Toledo?"*

*I shook my head nervously.*

*"Well, they do." She nodded. "I been thinkin' about goin' over there to volunteer while you was in school all week long. Help the boys and girls out. I guess that's just what I'll do."*

*Then she turned back to the stove and started stirring the gravy again. I allowed myself to give a wary smile.*

*"Maybe you can go with me?" She suggested gently.*

*"Maybe..."*

*"Who's this boy?" Oma didn't let my hesitance overtake the conversation. "Do I know him? I should. I know everybody around here. Better not be one them Kelly boys. Ugly, Irish assholes."*

*"Are you ever going to be nice to them?" I teased. "Besides, they're all a lot older than me, Oma."*

*"I'll sit up in my coffin to spit at them if they show up at the funeral." Oma waggled her head as she cooked. "Who's the boy, damnit?"*

*"Luc-Lucas Barkley?" I stammered, suddenly very nervous.*

*Oma turned to me again, the spoon in her hand dripping gravy onto the floor. She didn't notice.*

*"That Jackson Barkley's grandson?" She asked quickly. "The one who plays football?"*

*I nodded jerkily.*

*Oma cackled and then noticed the gravy on the floor.*

*"Shit." She admonished herself before retrieving a paper towel to clean up the mess she had made.*

*Oma bent down to wipe up the gravy.*

*"Well," She grunted as she wiped, "Lucas is a good kid. But Jackson Barkley will shit his britches knowin' that his grandson is..."*

*She glanced up at me, stopping herself from saying whatever it was she was going to say. I stared at her.*

*"I wasn't gonna say nothin' too bad." She waved me off as she stood up and deposited the soiled paper towel in the trashcan. "I don't even know if Jackson will give a shit, to be honest."*

*"Oma..."*

*"Well, I'm sorry." She snapped, but she didn't have the heart to put the full force of her sass behind it. "I was just gonna say he 'had a little sugar in his tank' is all."*

*"It's not the most offensive thing you've ever said," I mumbled, and Oma shot a squinty-eyed look over her shoulder, silencing me.*

*The cellar door creaked open suddenly, and I looked over to see Ernst come out, looking around as though to make sure that there were no visitors. Once it was clear to him that it was just the three of us, his eyes locked onto me.*

*"Good morning, Ernst." I beamed.*

*"Good-mornin', Rob." He smiled back.*

*Ernst exited the cellar and shut the door gently behind himself as Oma gave him a "good mornin'" over her shoulder. Ernst returned the sentiment and sauntered over to the table to stand beside me, his head barely higher than my lap in my seated position.*

*"Didja sleep well, Rob?"*

*I didn't respond verbally. Instead, I smiled and scooted my seat back, making the legs scrape against the linoleum unpleasantly. Ernst didn't hesitate as he climbed up and sat on my knee. Oma cast a disapproving glance over her shoulder and shook her head as she began piling a plate high with the heavenly concoction she had whipped up for breakfast. Doing her best to not slap the plate down on the table, Oma set the breakfast in front of Ernst and me before shaking her head once more. I picked up my fork while Ernst grabbed a strip of my bacon and began nibbling at it happily. It had taken a few years for him to sit at the table with me, under the watchful eye of Oma. He had become less fearful of showing impropriety when it became clear that Oma wouldn't say anything while I was around. Ernst was my friend. Oma let it slide.*

*"You two are thicker than thieves, ain'tcha?" Oma stated blandly as she made her own plate.*

*Ernst nibbled nervously and looked up at me, and I just gave him a wink.*

*Lucas never liked meeting anywhere we might be seen by the other kids we went to school with each day. Being a naïve, mostly sheltered country kid myself, I assumed it was because I was a theater kid, and he was a football player. It was a personal "head-slapping" moment for me when I realized the actual reason behind his*

*secretive behavior. Of course, when Lucas and I had first started hanging out, I thought we were becoming just friends. I had known that I was gay…or, at least, I had a pretty good idea. Lucas hadn't indicated that he was gay when we started becoming friends, so it never crossed my mind that anything besides friendship was developing. Later, when we kissed for the first time, I had an Oprah "Ah-ha Moment." Obviously, he was gay—or gay-ish, which were the only LGBT terms I understood at the time—and wanted more than friendship. Knowing this, he wanted to keep the fact that we hung out a secret, even though I was not out of the closet to anyone except Oma at the time. I had just been too dense to understand what was unfolding before my very eyes. Lucas, of course, had been much quicker at figuring things out than I had been. He had always been smarter than me.*

*"We could go down to the bowling alley," I suggested as we walked along the shore of Lake Erie, beyond the woods bordering Oma's property. Lucas was skipping rocks sporadically, and I was collecting interesting pebbles in my pocket. We were fifteen and should have had more exciting things to do. "We could go see a movie or something. Ernst said he would show us some more tricks if you want."*

*Oma wasn't aware, but I had introduced Lucas to Ernst within the first days of becoming friends with him. I had known that he would be able to keep a secret. Just as I had suspected, and though Lucas had been gobsmacked by the appearance of a Kobold, he had kept his lips shut. He and Ernst had taken to each other after Lucas' initial shock wore off, and they always talked at least a little bit every time Lucas showed up to hang out. Lucas stayed clear of the house, though. He hadn't wanted Oma to see him. We always met at the edge of the yard or down by the lake. But Ernst would always at least say "hello" to Lucas before the two of us left to do...whatever it was we decided to do.*

*Lucas' reply was slow to come, "I like just being out here."*

*"Okay." I shrugged and bent down to grab a rock so black and shiny that it looked like obsidian.*

*Shoving the rock in my pocket, I turned to watch Lucas skip another one across the eerily calm surface of the lake.*

*"The play was really good," Lucas stated as he slid his hands into his pockets and stared out at the lake.*

*"Thanks." I smiled widely. "Oma took me to Toledo afterward last night. We got burgers and milkshakes and saw a movie and...it was kind of cool, I guess."*

*Lucas smiled, still looking out at the lake.*

*"I mean, it was kind of stupid, too." I backtracked. "I kind of just wanted to hang out with the cast. Grandmas, right?"*

*I sighed as though the weight of the world was on my world-weary fifteen-year-old shoulders. Cool kids don't feel happy about spending time with their parents or grandparents.*

*"I think it's cool."*

*Surveying Lucas' face for hints of a lie as he looked out at the lake, I found none.*

*"It was cool," I confirmed.*

*"Mrs. Wagner seems really nice."*

*"You never come inside..."*

*"I know. You were an amazing Professor Harold Hill."*

*"When in Rome."*

*"Ohio?"*

*"Close enough."*

*"Don't let an Iowan hear you say that." Lucas laughed. "They'll be fit to be tied over in I-Oh-Way."*

*"We're both going to be in trouble with a capital 'T.'" I teased.*

*Lucas smiled crookedly as he turned his gaze from the sun-sparkling water and looked at me. I did my best not to swallow down whatever it was that was making my belly feel the way it felt as he looked at me. His blonde hair seemed to practically glow in the spring sun. His eyes looked even more like jade than they usually did. Puberty was having its way with Lucas—in all the best ways. His jaw was becoming sharper, stronger. His baby fat was being shed, and days playing football was making him lean and muscular. But none of that accounted for what hid behind the jade of his eyes. Kindness can be exercised, but it can't be learned. Lucas was intimately familiar with the concept.*

*"You're really funny."*

*I shrugged.*

*"What does that mean?" Lucas mimicked my shrug with a small chuckle.*

*"I don't know." I had to keep myself from shrugging again.*

*Lucas stared at me for a moment before turning to walk along the shore of the lake again. I followed silently, my hands still in my pockets. Suggesting more activities we could do instead of nothing came to mind, but I let it go. Spending time with Lucas at the lake had actually become my favorite activity very quickly. I just didn't want him to get bored with it.*

*"Are you coming to the football game on Friday?"*

*"I guess," I said, "I mean, I always do, right? Everyone does."*

*We both chuckled.*

*"Do you usually watch the game...or do you ignore it like everyone else?"*

*"I watch."*

*He glanced out at the lake quickly then gave an upward nod.*

*"Do you...I mean, you cheer for me, right?"*

*I gave him a nudge with my shoulder as we walked.*

*"Obviously."*

*He smiled, his eyes down.*

*"Grandpa cheers really loudly, so if I can single anyone out in the crowd, it's usually him."*

*"I guess I'll have to cheer louder." I shrugged, regardless of my desires.*

*"You don't really like sports, do you?"*

*"Honestly?"*

*"Yeah."*

*"No," I said. "Not really."*

*"But you still go to the football games?"*

*"Something to do on a Friday night, right?"*

*"You could go to the 'bowling alley or the movies,'" He teased.*

*Again, I was shrugging.*

*"Why do you keep coming?"*

*How to respond to the question evaded me as we walked along the shore, the perfectly still water and lack of breeze making the silence palpable. Initially, I started going to football games because that's just what high school kids did. They went to football games and socialized and flirted and hung out. Sometimes they actually even cheered for the team. Over time, I realized that football was no more exciting than any other sport I despised. I enjoyed socializing with my friends...mostly...but I was also incredibly bored at the games, too. In sophomore year, when Lucas started playing, though, things changed.*

*The blonde, good-looking guy—though I wasn't entirely sure how I felt about that at the time—that I vaguely knew from classes and the hallways, caught my eye. It made the games more tolerable. After the very first game, I made sure to say "hello" to him in the hallways anytime I saw him. I'd smile at him in classes if I didn't actually talk to him. A friendship slowly began to form. And then Mr. Barkley had brought Lucas out to hang out that one day...and we became...friend? Lucas glanced at me as though he would add a follow-up question, so I knew that answering his first question was important; otherwise, he'd think of ten more.*

*"Well," I said, "I have to support you, don't I?"*

*"I guess."*

*"I guess?" I feigned a chuckle. "I don't have to come, do I?"*

*"No."*

*"Then show some gratitude, damnit." I genuinely laughed.*

*But the laugh was cut off when Lucas turned to me, took my face in his hands and pulled my face into his. My eyes opened wide in shock as his lips connected with mine. Lucas' eyes were closed firmly with concentration and determination. The kiss itself was too wet, too firm, too...perfect. After a moment, I let my eyes close as Lucas held his mouth to mine, though that was all the kiss really consisted of—two pairs of lips pressed together firmly and wetly. When Lucas finally pulled away, I let my eyes flutter open to find him staring fearfully at me. His hands didn't leave my face.*

*"You didn't pull away."*

*I shook my head.*

*"Oh, shit." He swallowed as his hands slid from my face, obviously concerned at my lack of verbal response. "I didn't...look, let's just...Rob, I didn't mean to—"*

*I ignored his sputtering and reached up to lay my hand against his cheek, letting my thumb jerkily brush over his cheek. His words, fortunately, ceased, which gave me the perfect opportunity to lean in and kiss him back. Lucas shut his eyes forcefully, eagerly, as I eased my face to his. The corner of my mouth turned up in amusement as I closed my eyes and gently pressed my lips to his. Lucas seemed to melt into me as I kissed him, my thumb learning to slide along his cheek more expertly as I did so. The kiss didn't last long—I didn't want to attempt more than a simple kiss. When I pulled away, Lucas' eyes stayed closed several moments longer than mine, as though he had lost himself in the moment, but when they finally opened, they looked greener than ever.*

*"You like me, too?"*

*I nodded.*

*"Was the kiss...okay?" He looked away but made no effort to pull his face away from my hand.*

*"The first one or the second one?"*

*"Either."*

*"They were both perfect."*

*Then Lucas was amateurishly pulling my face to his again right there on the shore of Lake Erie, pressing his lips against mine. It was perfect, too.*

*"Is that what you think?" I spun on my heels to growl at Oma.*

*"Of course, I do." She snapped back. "I think you're not thinkin' with your head. You're usin' another organ."*

*In case I was confused, she tapped a finger against her chest. At least she hadn't tapped her crotch. I rolled my eyes and turned back around, headed for the living room. Oma would never let me storm out on her, especially during an argument, but I was sixteen. What sixteen-year-old hasn't jumped on a huff and rode it away when the mood struck them? I hadn't even stepped from the kitchen into the living room when Oma snapped at me.*

*"Where the hell do you think you're goin'?"*

*"To my room!" I screamed over my shoulder.*

*"The day pigs fly!" She bellowed.*

*Chair legs scraping against linoleum sounded, and I picked up my pace slightly as I made my way to the stairs and started up them in a sturdy march. If I could only get up the stairs, down the hall, and to my room, maybe I could lock the door and avoid Oma. Of course, if I thought a locked door would keep Oma from continuing the argument, I was dumber than dirt.*

*"You swivel your ass and get back down here!" Oma shouted at me from the bottom of the stairs.*

*I turned on the landing to glower at her.*

*"No."*

*"Don't you sass me." She put her hands on her hips and glared up at me.*

*"It's my life!" I snapped. "And just like everything else, you're telling me how to do everything!"*

*"Robbie," Oma looked at me through squinty eyes, "this isn't about gettin' your driver's license or a curfew. This is about your damn life."*

*"Right." I nodded firmly down at her. "My life. Not yours. Not Lucas'. Just mine. I can do with it what I like."*

*Oma crossed her arms over her breast and cocked an eyebrow at me as she looked up at me standing on the landing.*

*"You're plannin' to do a damn fool thing, is what you're plannin'." Oma waggled her head. "You think you understand everything. Just like every other dumbass teenager. Well, you don't know shit, Robbie."*

*"What don't I know?" I demanded. "I know exactly what this means, and you're trying to convince me that I don't understand."*

*"You don't understand, damnit!" She replied sharply. "Your mother and father—"*

*"Where are mom and dad?" I looked around dramatically. "I think the only people who get to be involved in an argument are the ones here, don't you?"*

*"More fuckin' sass." She rolled her eyes.*

*"I've made my decision." I crossed my own arms over my chest.*

*"You're goin' to let yourself get kilt because—for what?" Oma demanded. "What's that gonna do for any-damn-one?"*

*"What's the alternative, Oma? Tell me that. You knew—**you knew**—this day was coming, and*

*you just stayed silent. The only time you've ever stayed silent—"*

*"Don't you—"*

*"—and now I have exactly two choices, and you're telling me which one to make without even discussing it!" I bellowed. "This isn't about you. It's about me, Oma!"*

*"It's about everyone!"*

*"Why'd I have to be born?" I screamed down the stairs at her. "If I hadn't been born, I wouldn't have to deal with any of this!"*

*Oma's eyes grew wide as a hand went to her chest.*

*"I wish I didn't know any of this shit!" I continued. "I wish I wasn't here! I wish I didn't know what I know! I wish I didn't have to look at you! I wish I didn't have to worry about Lucas! I wish Ernst was safe! I wish I had more time—"*

*"Shut up, Robbie!" Oma hissed, her foot rising to the first step of the stairs.*

*My mouth stayed open, but I didn't say another word. Oma's hand was on the newel post cap and the other on her chest. She glanced down at the floor fearfully, then up at me desperately.*

*"Don't make wishes, Robbie. Not even in your own head," She pleaded. "You know better."*

*"Sorry." I snapped, but my heart wasn't in it. "I'm still learning all the rules."*

*"You think you're going to solve all of this with a wish?" She barked.*

*"It's better than your plan to feed me to the wolves." I barked back. "Almost literally!"*

*"It's only been eleven years since he was sent away last time, Robbie." Oma howled at me. "Eleven goddamn years since your daddy put him in the ground. He's too powerful for you."*

*"That's why I'm not going to face him!" I screamed, the glass panes in the front door shattering.*

*Oma jumped. I did not.*

*"I'll never face him," I added quietly, once the tinkling of broken glass tapered off. "If I can avoid it."*

*Oma just stared up at me in shock.*

*Then I stomped the rest of the way up the stairs. Once I'd made my way to my bedroom, I made sure to slam the door as hard as I could. The whole house shook.*

*"Stay down," Lucas whispered as we huddled behind the bleachers.*

*"Okay."*

*We had almost been seen. I managed to peek over my shoulder as I crouched there in the dirt under the bleachers in the football stadium. Jason and the other football players were walking through the bleachers, searching. I knew who they were searching for, but I wasn't sure why.*

*"Why are they looking for you?"*

*Lucas looked over at me, his eyes locking onto mine.*

*"They still want me to join them."*

*My eyes grew wide.*

*"But you're not—"*

*"It doesn't matter."*

*"Why would Jason-fucking-Morris think you'd want anything to do with them, Lucas?" I whispered. "They're assholes."*

*Lucas chewed at his lip.*

*"You're obviously so not."*

*He gave a nervous smile.*

*"You're not—you're not going to join them, are you?"*

*"I'd rather die."*

*"I don't want that either." I teased.*

*"They're going to make my life—our lives—really hard, Rob." Lucas sighed. "I'm so sorry I got you into this."*

*"We both cause trouble for each other." I gave him a crooked smile.*

*Lucas returned the look.*

*"Trouble won't stop us, though." He stared into my eyes. "Right?"*

*"If it does—it'll only be temporary."*

*I held out my pinkie.*

*It was a juvenile gesture.*

*Lucas stared down at my pinkie with a wicked smile. Then he pulled me into him and smothered my mouth with his. When he pulled back, he was still smiling.*

*"That's how I make promises."*

*"I like your method."*

***"LUCAS!"***

*Lucas was out of breath, and his fingers were laced through mine as we slid to a stop*

*behind the tree. The moon was dark, and I could barely see any stars through the skeletal canopy above us. Somehow, I felt like the moon was watching us, tracking our movements through the woods. Hopefully, it knew how to keep its mouth shut. I pushed Lucas against the tree as he tried to control his breathing and not pant loudly so as to not give away where we were. How was I breathing normally, and the football player was out of breath after our jaunt through the cold, slumbering woods?*

***"ROBERT!"***

*"Oh, shit." Lucas hissed, his eyes fearful.*

*"It'll be okay." I grabbed his face between my hands and made him look at me. "I promise you it'll be okay."*

*Lucas looked into my eyes, the fear slowly melting away.*

*"You can run." I pleaded with him. "Run to the lake. Then keep running along the shore until you get to the road. Keep running until you get home."*

*"I won't leave you."*

*"This is only going to end one way, Lucas," I whispered desperately. "I don't want you to see it."*

*"I can't let you do this alone."*

*"I won't hate you if you run."*

*"You will eventually."*

*"Do you think I'll love you forever if you stay?" I managed to tease though I was terrified as the sound of crisp, cold leaves being stomped on sounded in the distance. "Is that why you're doing this?"*

*"I know you'll love me forever." He responded, then kissed me roughly.*

*It was a quick kiss, but perfect like every kiss that came before it. Lucas pulled back, his hands on the side of my face.*

*"Everything is temporary," Lucas stated firmly. "Everything."*

*"Everything." I nodded. "Are you sorry?"*

*"I'll never be sorry."*

*"Me either."*

*"Can we make it back to the house?" Lucas swallowed hard. "Before...will I just slow you down?"*

*"I want you with me." I grabbed his face in my hands. "I want you to be the last thing I see."*

*Lucas' eyes started to leak.*

*"I'm going to miss you."*

*"I'll miss you more."*

*"What if—what if it's not temporary?"*

*"Hey!" I whisper-hissed, holding his face firmly in my hands so he had to look at me. "Every-fucking-thing is temporary. Except us. Except us, Lucas. I promise you that."*

*Lucas stared into my eyes, two trails of tears winding down his face.*

*"I believe you."*

*I nodded.*

*"Are you ready?" I asked.*

*Lucas took a shaky breath, doing his best to stop the tears from escaping his eyes. Finally, he steadied himself, resolve settling on his face. He nodded.*

*"I can do this."*

*"I will do this."*

*"You'll come back."*

*A voice in the back of my head wasn't so sure.*

*"I will come back."*

*"Promise?"*

*"Yes." I nodded once. "I promise."*

*"I love you." Lucas whimpered. "Just in case I haven't told you enough. In case I never get to again."*

*"I love you, too."*

*I kissed Lucas again, then laced my fingers through his, and we raced away from the tree towards the house.*

*The room was cold.*

*Bitterly cold.*

*And I had no memory of the room.*

*But that didn't keep me from opening my eyes to find that I was lying on the bed in the middle of the room.*

*It wasn't apparent at first, due to my confusion at waking up in a strange room, chilled to my bones, but I wasn't even in Lucas' house. In fact, I wasn't sure whose house I was in, actually. The room did not look familiar—but it looked somewhat familiar at the same time. Maybe because it looked like a child's bedroom—the dark shape of an overflowing bookcase in the corner. A desk for homework along one wall. A toy chest that was overflowing. Cartoon sheets of some kind that I had kicked off in my sleep.*

*With my child-sized feet.*

*I gazed down at my body only to find that I was not staring at my body but that of a child—or a very young teen. Maybe a tween? This revelation should have sent a shock of terror up my spine, but*

*I was getting used to the odd things in my life. Instead of screaming out in shock or panicking in any way, I sat up cautiously and swiveled my hips to let my legs dangle off of the side of the bed. Giving a quick glance around the room, looking for any sign of danger, I lowered myself to the floor.*

*Icy cold floorboards slapped against my feet, and I winced, though I made no noise. It was dark, I had no idea where I was, and there was no way for me to know if there was anyone else in the house. Would someone come to investigate if they heard me? And if someone did come to investigate, would they be dangerous? Harm me in some way? I let my feet adjust to the cold of the floorboards as I scanned the room slowly with my eyes.*

*Just a typical tween's room.*

*Nothing unusual.*

*Other than the darkness.*

*Nothing looks normal in the dark.*

*As I stood there, my feet adjusting to the cold and my eyes adjusting to the darkness, my ears began to pick up the voices.*

*Beyond the door positioned at the opposite side of the room, someone was talking. Low and rumbly, the voices sounded muffled and hollow. My feet began to move without me willing it, and I found myself being drawn towards the bedroom door. The cold was pervasive, making my feet—well, the feet I now had—feel like blocks of ice. It pushed through the cotton of the pajamas I was wearing. It slid over and around my body, doing its best to compel me back into bed. To forget the voices and the door.*

*Suddenly, I found myself in front of the door, my hands reaching out to brace myself against it as my ear moved towards the cold, smooth wood. My ear connected with the icy surface, trying to hear the voices better. To try and figure out what it was they were saying.*

*The voices became louder with my ear pressed against the door, but I still couldn't make out what it was they were saying. After a few moments, listening to what sounded like two voices quarreling or, maybe, debating, I crouched down next to the doorknob. I leveled my eye to the keyhole and looked through into the room beyond.*

*What I saw...was I really seeing this?*

*In the room beyond, seemingly lit by fire or candlelight, was a pile of raw bones, gleaming white and splattered with blood. Sat upon what could only be described as the "throne" of bones was a hooded figure.*

*I knew that figure.*

*As if he knew I was watching, the hooded figure's head turned towards the door.*

*Red eyes peered out of the hood and into the keyhole.*

*Then I was falling backward.*

*"Why do you always read this book?" I asked, pointing at the book open in Oma's lap at my bedside.*

*I was snuggled down in the covers as snow fell outside of my bedroom window, blanketing the ground outside in knee-high fluff.*

*"I want you to remember this story, Robbie." She replied and shifted in her chair, trying not to lose her place in the book.*

*"Why do you keep it under the bookcase?" I asked.*

*"Well—"*

*"And why don't I ever get to read it myself?"*

*"Because—"*

*"Was that mom's and dad's book?"*

*"Why do you have so many questions?" Oma barked, though her eyes twinkled. "It's just a damn book. It only opens a certain way and only lets certain people tell its story. Yes. It belonged to your mom and dad. And I want to read it to you as often as possible, so you remember the story. Okay?"*

*I shrugged, smiling.*

*"Good." Oma nodded once. "Now, where were we?"*

*"You were telling me about the witch that The Oracle and The Guardian found who was going to defeat the bad guy," I replied.*

*"Right," Oma said. "Okay, so..."*

"Are you Robbie, sugar?" I looked up from my plate of nachos at the Red Rooster Tavern.

It was only a little after three o'clock, and I was supposed to be meeting Lucas for a snack after school. As usual, football practice was causing him to run late, so I had started without him, happy to eat nachos, and wait until he was done. Mr. Kelly—the Kelly's son who had taken over the tavern when his parents left, and word had was about to sell the tavern to someone else *at his father's behest—let the kids from the school come in for lunches and mid-afternoon snacks, but once six o'clock came, he shooed them all away. The cocktail hours had approached for the adults. When I looked up at the person who had asked me if I was Robbie, I saw a man I'd never seen before standing there. Catching sight of him immediately brought a smile to my face, though his appearance made me nervous.*

*Dark skinny jeans, fashionable, yet cheap, heels, a chunky burnt orange sweater that hung off one shoulder, a scarf in contrasting pink, and large Audrey Hepburn like glasses adorned his lithe frame. A purse big enough to hold A through F in the encyclopedia was slung over one forearm. He looked down at me, a broad smile that showed his immaculately bright, white teeth shined down at me.*

*'My people.' I had thought.*

*"That's me."*

*I had almost said it like it was a question.*

*"Oh, good." He threw his head back as if completely exhausted and slid into the booth across from me.*

*Immediately, I looked around, wondering what people would think if they saw my teenage self with a man...like this. He was definitely waving the Pride Flag with every ounce of his being. My eyes grew wide as I realized that everyone else in the Red Rooster Tavern seemed frozen in place. Immediately, I glanced over at the man sitting across from me.*

*"Wha—"*

*"Just a little magic." The man fluttered his fingers through the air with a cackle, then removed his sunglasses. "It won't hurt them none, baby."*

*I couldn't help but smile, though I was alarmed to hear someone besides Oma talk about magic in front of me.*

*"Who..."*

*"Carlos, baby." He held out his hand, palm down over the table towards me. "But I prefer 'Carlita' if you don't mind. I ain't got the wig on today, and the dress is at the dry cleaners, but that's just how these things happen."*

*I took her hand, giving it a gentle shake.*

*"Okay. Carlita." I slowly nodded. "I am Robbie."*

*"Good, good." She wriggled her fingers through the air again as though trying to remember something. "Now, listen, I don't want to be here any longer than I have to—I got my own matters to tend to, obviously."*

*"Okay?"*

*"Tell Esther Jean Wagner—"*

*I froze at the sound of my grandmother's name. This woman knew Oma? Why had she never mentioned her before?*

*"—that the man in the black hooded cloak is coming."*

*My eyes grew wide as I gasped.*

*"She told me that she had done talked to you about him."*

*"You mean Bloo—"*

*"No, child." Carlita hushed me. "Don't say his name this close to his return. Why speed things up, ya' know?"*

*A hand to my chest, I just nodded, my breathing increasing in speed as my heart thumped against my chest.*

*"He's comin', baby. It's time." Carlita reached out and patted my other hand that was atop the table. "I always hate this part, delivering*

*the news to the next witch, but, well, that's what an oracle is for, isn't it?"*

*"Oracle?" I gasped again, then leaned forward, forgetting my rapid breathing and thumping heart. "The Oracle? From the story?"*

*"It's obviously not just a story." She leveled me with her eyes. "And everything Esther Jean Wagner's been preparing you for...well, it's time, baby. You tell Esther Jean that. Now. I gotta go. Things to see and people to do."*

*Carlita slid out of the booth and draped her purse handles over her forearm once again. Her sunglasses got pushed onto her face where they had been when she entered. Then she was stomping fashionably towards the door of the tavern as the people around me slowly started to come back to life.*

*"Wait!" I spun in the booth to look at her.*

*Carlita stopped just inside the tavern and turned her head to look at me, a smile coming to her face.*

*"If you're The Oracle...where's The Guardian?" I asked quickly.*

*Carlita just smiled.*

*"I have so many questions." I pleaded.*

*As if trying to think of something important, or trying to remember something, Carlita's head tilted back gently as she looked up at the ceiling, searching for words.*

*"You'll get a chance to ask them." She finally turned her head to answer me. "But it won't be for a while. This won't be the last time we meet, Robbie Wagner."*

*"Rob." I couldn't think of anything else to say.*

*"I'll try to remember that." She tapped her temple.*

*Then she was gone, the door swinging behind her and the people in the tavern coming to life like a snap.*

*"Are you sure you want to do this?" Lucas asked.*

*We were already naked, and he was on top of me, so I wanted to laugh at the timing of the question.*

*"Obviously." I nodded, my teeth biting into my lower lip.*

*The woods behind Oma's house were dark and creepy all around us. We had made our bed on a pile of leaves. It was so cold, especially naked.*

*"We don't have to." He whispered.*

*"I want to," I said eagerly. "I don't want to leave without doing this. Just in case—and as long as you want to, too."*

*"Just in case?" Lucas looked terrified. "You're coming back, Rob."*

*"I know." I nodded. "But this will make leaving easier."*

*Lucas kept himself propped over me with a hand on either side of my body digging into the cold ground. I could feel, against my thigh, that he wanted the same thing that I wanted.*

*"Say you'll come back."*

*"I'll come back."*

*"Promise?"*

*"Promise."*

*"We'll be together forever?"*

*"Even in death."*

*Lucas' body sank into mine. Under a nearly moonless sky, the stars already blotted out, we made love. And I wondered if I hadn't just lied to Lucas. What if I never came back?*

*"Fuck!" Lucas screamed as we slammed the door to the house behind us and threw both of our bodies against it. "They're right behind us, Rob!"*

*Lucas and I held ourselves against the door, digging our heels into the hardwood floor as the sound of wolves throwing themselves against the door sounded. We had passed Oma and Carlita as we ran through the woods towards the house. They had merely been standing there, watching us. Lucas had wanted to stop and scream for them to come help...but I had known that it would be pointless. They were meant to watch. Besides preparing me, those were their roles in this never-ending story. I had urged Lucas to continue running, to put as much distance between ourselves, Bloody Bones, and his wolves.*

*"I have to get to the cellar," I said, twisting the deadbolt, flipping the lock on the knob and sliding the chain in place. "Come on!"*

*"Rob." Lucas turned to look at me, his back still to the door.*

*"What?" I turned to look at him, my heart thundering, and my mind racing with the wish I had in my head. "What is it?"*

*"I don't want to watch you go." He said, his face a steel mask, though a single tear slid from his eye and over his cheek.*

*Simultaneously I hated and loved Lucas. I loved how much he didn't want me to go, but I hated how I would have to do what I had to do all on my own. When I saw a tear slide from his other cheek, I couldn't be mad any longer. I just wanted everything to be over.*

*"Okay." I nodded, trying to not shed any of my own tears.*

*Lucas stared at me, tears rolling down his cheeks, trying to figure out what to say. Suddenly, his eyes flicked away from mine, landing on something to my side.*

*"Ernst!" Lucas bellowed as the sound of more wolves throwing themselves against the door met our ears. "Ernst, we need your help!"*

*I turned to find my best friend at my side, looking up at me with wide, terrified eyes.*

*"Ernst." I sighed, no longer able to control my tears. "Hey."*

*"'Ello, Rob." He reached up to grab my hand.*

*"Ernst." Lucas continued. "Go with Rob. Don't let him be alone."*

*"Wha's 'appnin'?" Ernst looked up at me, the terror replaced by wonder.*

*"I'm going to make this all stop," I said, simply.*

*"I can't do it, Ernst," Lucas said, still bracing himself against the door as the chain rattled as the door was pounded on by wolves' bodies. "But I don't want him to be alone. Will you go with him?"*

*Ernst squeezed my hand, and a look of pride replaced all of the others.*

*"I'd be honored, Rob." He said.*

*I smiled down at him, trying to stop my tears but finding myself unable. I didn't want to leave Lucas, Ernst...I didn't want any of this.*

*"Go!" Lucas screamed as a green light started shining through the front windows of the house.*

*Gasping at the sight of the light and Lucas' form bathed in it, I pulled away from Ernst and ran over to my boyfriend. Quickly, I shoved my mouth over his. His lips accepted mine, and I felt the trail of tears on my cheek meld with the river of tears on his cheek. When I pulled back, Lucas looked more determined. I felt more determined.*

*"Even in death." He nodded.*

*"Even then." I nodded back.*

*"Go." He stated simply.*

*Pushing away from Lucas so that I couldn't second guess myself, I turned and ran towards the cellar door, grabbing Ernst's arm on the way. Together, we ran hand and hand through the living room into the kitchen, and I threw open the cellar door. The two of us dashed down the steps as more pounding sounded from above, and everything around us seemed to be glowing in a green light. Running directly to the edge of the well, I let go of Ernst's hand and climbed up on the wall of the well.*

*"Rob!" Ernst gasped. "Wha' are you doin'?"*

*I looked down at my friend.*

*"Stopping all of this," I said, simply.*

*"Don'!" He bellowed to be heard over the sounds upstairs. "Please, Rob!"*

*"I have to, Ernst." I felt tears flowing freely over my cheeks. "It's why I'm here. You know that."*

*Tears were flowing from Ernst's cheeks, too. I could see in his face that he wanted to say something, that he was trying to force himself to say something...but then his face turned into a steely mask like Lucas' had. He simply nodded at me.*

*"Thank you for making sure I wasn't alone," I said. "I love you, Ernst."*

*"I love you, too, Rob." He responded, his back straightening, bringing him to his full height—which wasn't that great. "An' I am proud to 'ave been yer friend.'"*

*"No prouder than I am to have been yours." I smiled as warmly as I could.*

*Then, before we could say anything else that would delay or stop me, I turned and gazed down at the well. The green light wasn't just coming from the windows upstairs...it was emanating out from the bottom of the well, too. I gazed down into its blinding depths and braced myself.*

*I wish...*

*I wish I could forget everything. I wish Bloody Bones was gone. I wish that Lucas, Ernst, and everyone I love could be safe again.*

*And then I was falling.*

*The world's largest lucky penny.*

*It was dark when my eyes opened once again. I was in my room, lying on my bed. I wasn't in my pajamas or under the covers. I was merely laying on top of the bed, fully clothed. The room was dark, and the moon and stars were twinkling*

*in the sky outside of my window. A quick glance over to my bedside table let me know that it was well after midnight.*

*A flash of a memory—Oma's hand on my forehead.*

*Whispered words.*

*I shook my head to clear my thoughts.*

*Why was I in bed like this? How did I get in bed? I didn't remember ever walking up to my room and going to sleep. I had gone to have nachos at The Red Rooster Tavern and...then...I didn't know.*

*Sitting up in my bed, I could sense that the house was deadly quiet. Oma must have already gone to bed. A shadow in the corner of my room moved. My head jerked to the side.*

*Was that...*

*I thought I saw a...little person?*

*A smile formed on my face at the thought. That was the most ridiculous thing ever. I was too old to be creeping myself out.*

*It's time to go.*

*The thought entered my head like a bullet.*

*So...I slid off of the bed.*

*Next to where my feet landed was a suitcase on wheels, the handle extended, ready to be wheeled away.*

*And that's what I did. I crept down the stairs, carrying the suitcase carefully the whole way, even stopping at Oma's closed bedroom door to make sure she truly was asleep. Then I went out the front door, locking it behind myself, walked across the porch, and down into the yard. Turning to give the house one last look, I gave a sigh. Point Worth just wasn't for me. I was meant for bigger things.*

*Hollywood.*

*California.*

*Not Podunk, Ohio.*

*I turned, let the suitcase fall to the ground, and wheeled it behind me as I walked towards the main road.*

*Did you see that?*

# Chapter 12

Oma, Lucas, and I stood inside the fence that surrounded the garden, staring down at the ground as Oma jabbed at it with a stick. Lucas was holding my hand, his body slumped against mine, leaning against me for strength. The rush of our memories being returned to us—in no particular order—had done a number on him. In all honesty, my knees still felt like they were jelly, and there was a pretty intense throbbing at the lower base of my skull above my spine. Getting memories back—*real memories*—and so many at one time, well, the human body just isn't meant to handle such a thing. The walk up the stairs from the cellar and out to the garden had been challenging.

Of course, I really had no one to blame but myself. Oma might have fucked with our memories some, after I jumped in the well the first time, and since I'd been back, but we had lost a lot of our real memories in the first place thanks to me. I was the one who had made three wishes and jumped into the well in the cellar—when it was still there—to use the power to defeat Bloody Bones. But like every witch that had come before me, I had failed to understand that no magic would ever be strong enough to defeat him for good. He was just as big a part of the magic of the lands we stood upon as anyone else.

"Made sure they was buried properly," Oma said, jabbing at the ground and avoiding my eyes.

"Respectful like. Me and the Kobolds saw to that, Rob."

"I'm sure you did your best." I had no fight in me now that I knew the truth.

"Your mom, well, she was really just collateral damage," Oma said quietly, staring at the ground. "Your daddy, he knew what was comin' for him. He just didn't realize it was comin' so soon. He met Carlita that mornin', while you was wakin' up and havin' breakfast…by the time he got to the house after talkin' to Carlita and bein' told he was comin', ole Red Eyes had done did what he did to your mother and was turnin' on you. Your daddy did his best to run Bloody Bones off…but he knew he had to face him in real battle. He knew he had to do what he was born to do."

"I see."

"Jesus in a gravy boat," Oma shook her head, "we had trained him like he was young. Just like all the others. But Bloody Bones never came when it was time. We thought maybe he was never comin'. Your daddy went on about his life. Got married. Had you…y'all was livin' pretty good. Then…poof. Bloody Bones decided to show up. It wasn't right. It wasn't fair. But it is what it is."

"It is that." I sighed, wrapping my arms around Lucas.

"So," I said, "I was born, and this ended up falling on me instead of some other distant relative simply because he decided to take a rest?"

"Essentially." Oma shrugged. "I suppose so. If he had come for your father when he should-a, well, we wouldn't be talkin' right now, Rob. But…well, you know the story of how Bloody Bones came to be. You know about the first witch. You know about how the magic to fight him was in her bloodline and the magic she used that made that well. You know your parents died that day—your mom protecting you—and your daddy doin' what he was born to do. You know I ain't your grandmother—"

"You're The Guardian," I said simply, unemotionally.

"Yes." She sighed and looked up at us. "By the time he came for your daddy, Carlita and I was about fed up with this shit. A witch defeats him, he goes away. Comes back, another witch defeats him. On and on and on. Ain't none of 'em ever been powerful enough to keep him in the ground for good or outright destroy him. Or send him straight back down to Hell."

"But—"

"Well," Oma interrupted me, "that ain't necessarily true. The first witch...well, she did it. He would-a stayed locked away for good, I imagine. If it weren't for that goddamn well. And then—"

"Why did the well just...pop up out of the round?"

"That I don't know." Oma shook her head. "Carlita and I have discussed that over...many, many years...and the best we can decide is that there was too much magic in The Witch—the first one—for these lands to contain. Or maybe she consciously did that knowing that there would be extra help in the future if he ever returned. But...like all humans...your ancestors was a greedy bunch. Usin' magic like Lake Erie is filled with it. They perverted and destroyed that well. By the time you came around, we knew there wasn't much left for you to use if the time came."

"Just enough to make things drag on a little longer." I nodded.

"Right." Oma nodded. "And I just lied to you."

"What?" Lucas whispered, standing up a little straighter next to me, though his hands stayed tightly around mine.

"I said the first witch was the only one that could've gotten rid of him for good," Oma explained. "That ain't necessarily true. When your daddy died putting that shitass back in the ground, and I came here to look after you, to train you, teach you...I saw a little of that first witch in you. I thought you could actually do what needed to be done—but in a more permanent way. We just had to keep you alive long enough for you to build up the strength to do it."

"So," I snorted, my eyes shutting as I smiled ruefully, "you taught me the story. You trained me how to use my magic, you told me about Bloody Bones. You let me find the well—put the idea in my head to wish things away so that Bloody Bones would get sealed away a bit longer, the pack of wolves he built with the help of The Council would back off once their leader wasn't there to lead...then you put the idea in my head to run away."

It wasn't asking questions. I was recounting my memories.

"That sums it up mostly." She agreed, letting the stick in her hand drop the ground so that she could cross her arms over her chest. "But then this one comes along."

Oma jabbed a finger at Lucas, and he actually twitched.

"While Bloody Bones was suckin' up magic out of the land and finding people to store it in until he was ready to rise and take it all back to use in his final attempt to stay in this world forever—to make it his...I don't know...*kingdom?*...he gave this one something special. Something he didn't mean to. He gave him the power to foresee things. Some folks around here ain't magical at all. Some is good with fire or levitating things. Some is good with potions or spells. But, Lucas here, he's special. I think he might have given him a bit of magic he didn't know enough about."

"What does that mean?" Lucas hissed his question.

"Well," Oma sighed, "your gift of foresight rivals that of Carlita—may she rest in peace. Way back when, when you two was becoming friends—"

"Which you and my grandfather arranged!" Lucas barked.

"Well, yeah." Oma shrugged again. "No sense in lyin'. When you two became friends—we saw a powerful witch and a powerful oracle. Carlita and I got to thinkin'...."

Lucas and I looked at each other, trying to figure things out. Finally, it dawned on me. I turned to Oma, an incredulous smile on my face.

"You thought that maybe I'd put this fucker in the ground for good, you and Carlita could, I don't know, *retire*, and Lucas and I could take over as guardian and oracle? Just in case he ever came back, and another witch needed to be found?"

Lucas snorted.

"That's about the size of it, yeah." Oma agreed, then her face turned angry. "But you was supposed to be gone *at least* another decade, damnit. You needed to mature and have your power grow. If you couldn't remember you had it, you wouldn't be usin' it for all them years. It could grow while he was stuck in the ground. But then you came back way before I expected it...and you started a whole chain of events, damnit. I tried runnin' you off. Made you think you was seein' things, hearin' things, savin' somethin' that looked like you form the lake, havin' Andrew attack you. Even negotiated with Jason and his pack to scare ya' a bit. They was more than happy to if it meant Bloody Bones would be destroyed, and maybe they could have their...*disease*...removed. Everyone worked together—except this one—since he didn't have his memories—to get you to leave."

"You pushed us together when I came back," I grumbled. "How did that serve your purpose?"

"Thought maybe you'd get scared off if you thought you was fallin' in love," Oma replied evenly. "You two was thick as thieves when you was young. I was quite impressed with the way you both worked together and put the dots together about the well and wishing things different. And, well, it brought me peace, knowing that when the time came—*ten years from now*—if you came back and banished Bloody Bones for good, and the two of you took over for me and Carlita—you'd have each other. You could spend the next millennia in each other's company. A love story for the ages."

I pulled my hand out of Lucas' and began a slow clap.

"Well done, asshole," I said to Oma.

"It wasn't a perfect plan." She hissed at me. "But we saw a chance to tip the tables in our favor. To get rid of this never-ending cycle of him comin' and goin'. We was tryin' to do right by you and your long family line, you asshole!"

"So, what now?" Lucas asked quickly, glancing over at me. "If Rob's here too early and Bloody Bones is off sucking up all the magic he pulled out of the land and stored away—"

"Yeah." Oma nodded. "I bet most the people in this town is dead already. He'll be heading this way soon, I spose."

"So, what do we do now?" Lucas demanded.

"He'll fight." Oma waved a hand at me. "He's gonna say he won't, but he will. It's what people like him do."

"People like him?" I grumbled.

"Witches." She spat. "Good people who do what they was born to do. Protect others. That's what people like you do. Because you was born to do it."

"Fuck you." I groaned.

She shrugged.

Something in my head, some tiny little voice was telling me something.

"So," I said, "he's been pulling magic out of the land and giving it to people. Giving them powers. Storing it away so one day, he could rise and take it all back and be more powerful than a witch could ever hope. Then he could squash that witch—me—easily and do what he's always wanted to do? Rule the world or some shit?"

"Spose."

"Where do you think he learned that idea?" I asked.

"What?" Oma and Lucas asked at the same time.

"People up here were using magic left by The Witch." I shrugged with a snort. "Maybe he got the idea of borrowing magic from that. Ya' think?"

"It's possible." She sniffed.

"But—" Lucas began.

"And did it ever occur to you," I interrupted him, "that maybe the first witch created the well to create balance?"

Lucas turned to me, a shocked expression on his face. Even Oma turned to me, concern etched all over her face.

"There's magic in the lands." I waved my arms around wildly. "Where he gets his power. Maybe the witch put the well full of magic there to create balance—that's what kept him in the ground. People siphoning from it, creating imbalance...he started siphoning and storing away his own. He knew the day would come that the well would run dry, and the scales would tip. You put the idea in my head to use the well—*my whole family had been doing it after all*—and wish him away. Then you confused me into using it a second time to implant more fake memories in my head when I got back. That was the last of it. There was no more balance. As soon as that well went dry, he's been digging his way up, lady."

Oma whispered something.

"What?" I barked.

"As above, so below," Oma repeated but not much louder or more clearly. "One of the first rules of magic."

"I don't know what that means," Lucas waved her off and turned to me, "Rob, what are we going to do?"

He took my face in his hands, turning my eyes from Oma to his.

"We know everything now." He said. "What are we going to do?"

"The only way to seal him back in the ground," I stared at Lucas for a moment, "would be to create another well. Create balance."

For several breaths, Lucas stared into my eyes.

"That would do it." Oma offered with a sigh.

Suddenly, a realization came to Lucas.

"No!" He demanded, his hands clenching at me. "You're not going to do that, Rob! No!"

"What other choice do we have?" I put my hands on his shoulders. "It's either all of us die, or...or..."

"That would leave me and her!" Lucas jabbed a finger at Oma, but his eyes stayed on mine. "You wouldn't be saving much, Rob. Everyone in this town is likely dead, having been drained by him. Taking the magic back will kill a person, right? Right?"

He was talking to Oma.

"I reckon so." She said, chewing at the side of her mouth. "But, I ain't goin' door to door to find out."

Lucas turned back to me.

"You can't sacrifice yourself just for us." Lucas shook his head. "I won't let you."

"I'm not sacrificing myself for the two of you," I said, placing a hand on his cheek. "I'm doing it for you. And the rest of the people in the world. I mean...do you think he's going to stop at Point Worth? That he'll be happy with that?"

"Rob..." Lucas groaned.

"Give me options." I offered to him. "Tell me what else can work. I'm willing to listen."

"There ain't no other way," Oma said sharply. "You meet him in battle, and you defeat him. Or he defeats you."

"Shut up!" Lucas barked at Oma, shocking me, but pleasantly. "What happens then, Rob? Huh? You seal him away; we get a new well...then someone else comes along and uses the power?

Then another? And another? Until it's all gone in a few centuries, and he comes back? Then what?"

"Maybe someone in my bloodline will still be around..." I hadn't thought of that.

"If you can't destroy him, you can't let yourself be destroyed." Lucas shook his head. "This is an impossible problem."

"How can he be destroyed, Lucas?" I asked him, pleaded with him. "As long as there is magic up here, there's...Bloody Bones."

The ground shook. Oma gasped, and Lucas grimaced.

"That ain't supposed to happen," Oma mumbled. "Bastard already crawled up out of Hell."

"Again," I snorted, "totally shocked that the portal to Hell was in this town."

Lucas gave a tight smile as the ground settled. We looked into each other's eyes as Oma stood in the middle of the garden, looking around as though she might come up with a solution. Or maybe she was looking for a place to bury me if my plan didn't work. Who was to say? Lucas stared at me, different emotions flashing across his face in succession, as though he was trying to think of something to say—or maybe how to say it.

"What is it?" I asked softly.

"Rob," Lucas said, "I saw you coming."

"Point Worth was on fire," I replied. "And I'm a fireman."

"And I saw how this ends."

"I know."

"I don't know what comes after...but I didn't see you die." Lucas said. "I saw...I saw..."

"What?" I asked, leaning in and kissing his lips softly. "What is it, babe?"

"I saw myself die." Lucas swallowed hard. "Not you."

I'd never been a wordsmith or someone who could eloquently describe my feelings in a way that would sound poetic. So, I had no way to describe the feeling of my heart dropping from my chest like a rollercoaster towards my feet while it felt like someone punched me in the gut simultaneously. Lucas' revelation about what he had seen was a one-two assault on my body and mind. All I could do was stare at him dumbly as my entire body went numb, and my heart decided that it was going on vacation.

"I died," Lucas said. "Not you. That's how this ends. At least...that's part of it. I can't see past my death."

"That's not true." I shook my head. "You're lying. That serves no purpose in solving our problem. How do you even think telling me that is going to change my mind about this? You dying won't stop Bloody Bones."

The ground shivered beneath our feet again.

"Ooooh," Oma waggled her head, not caring about the words Lucas and I were sharing, "he is comin', and he is pissed."

"All I'm saying, Rob," Lucas ignored her, "is that you can't save me—if that's why you're choosing to do what you think you have to do. I'm going to die. So...if you're doing this, only do it if you're doing it for everyone else. Not me. It won't help me."

"Stop it." I shoved him gently, though I didn't let him fall out of my personal space. "Stop fucking saying that."

"Do you want me to lie?" He sniffled.

"No, I just—"

"There has to be another way, Rob." Lucas stopped me. "Nowhere in my vision did I see you die saving me. If you are supposed to do that, I would have seen it happen before my death. I didn't see that."

"That doesn't mean that I'm not supposed to fight him."

"Maybe there is still enough magic left in the lands." Lucas offered quickly as the ground shook again, but harder. "If he can do it, maybe you can take magic from the land, too? Use his own tricks to defeat him and lock him away? If you used everything that's left and stuff him back in the ground, send him to Hell permanently with all of that magic, maybe that will work?"

"Will that save you?"

He shrugged then shivered.

"How can I know what the right thing to do is now, damnit?" I winced. "How do I know what can save you? If I do what was in my head all along, obviously, you die. But how are we to know what will happen if I change my mind about how to defeat him?"

"Ya' can't change your mind," Oma stated.

"What?" Lucas and I both turned our heads to snap at her.

"Ya' can't use the magic in the land." She reiterated. "He's carrying it all with him. Do you think the grounds shakin' for fun? That sumbitch is stompin' this way and sendin' us a warnin'. He's loaded for bear, and there's nothin' you can do about it but do what's always been done."

I didn't like it, but Oma had a point. Turning back to Lucas, I took his face in my hands.

"There is only one way," I told him in a hushed tone. "How do you die? Maybe if I—"

As if knowing this was the most imperfect time, a wolf's howl filled the air, making Lucas and I both jump as I stopped talking immediately. Oma sighed and turned to us, giving us a look that said: "Well, shit." As a threesome, though Oma was standing a few yards away, we turned, looking off in the direction from which the sound came. Our eyes landed on the tree line of the woods, off in the direction of Lake Erie. At first, I saw nothing but darkness and the trees that helped to create that darkness.

Then there were a pair of red, glowing eyes peeking out of the tree line, about waist high. Then another pair. Another pair. Then another. And another. Five pairs of eyes stared out of the darkness of the woods in our direction. Finally, a new pair of glowing, red eyes joined the bunch, but much higher than the others. Lucas squeezed my hand as we all stared towards the glowing, red eyes in the distance. We watched as one wolf emerged from the darkness, then another...until five wolves were standing just outside of the tree line, staring us down, muzzles pulled back, fangs bared.

Without having to be told, I knew the wolf in the middle was Jason. The pairs on either side of him were what remained of his functioning pack. They all stood there on all fours, snarling at us, fangs bared and eyes glowing, ready to tear us limb from limb if they could. The three of us waited, just like them, as the sixth pair of glowing red eyes stepped out of the darkness of the woods. But they weren't shrouded by a hood any longer. Bloody Bones had pulled back his cloak, exposing himself finally. A gleaming white skull, smeared in rust-colored stains and dripping blood, bony teeth and fangs bared, red eyes staring out at us, Bloody Bones was no longer hiding himself away.

"Well," Oma looked over her shoulder us, "I'm completely shocked by this turn of events. Are y'all?"

Lucas gave a whimpering groan as I glared at her.

Then the wolves were charging at us.

# Chapter 13

Three things began to happen simultaneously, but not at the same rate of speed as each other. Out of the corner of my eye, I saw Oma walking away, going to the far side of the fenced-in area of the garden, getting herself out of harm's away. Bloody Bones began walking in an arc towards the other side of the garden so that he would be out of this part of the fight and watch as well. If his wolves could do his work and save him the trouble, that was good enough for him. He just wanted me dead so that he could continue on with his plans to rule over the lands once again. Thirdly, I felt Lucas step a foot away from me, his hand tightening on mine. As the wolves charged us, getting closer and closer, Lucas raised his arm, pointing it directly at the wolves, and I felt a tingle start in my back, move over my shoulder blade, and down my arm.

A fireball shot from Lucas' palm and flew at the wolves just as they jumped in unison over the fence. Four wolves yipped and fumbled as the wolf on the left side of the pack burst into flames and fell to the ground, motionless. All four of the wolves seemed to be rethinking their tactic as their forward momentum halted so that they could glance at their fallen pack member. I wasn't going to give them an opportunity to regroup. Like Lucas, I held my hand up angrily and shot a fireball at the wolf on the right. The fire washed over him, and the other three wolves jumped back, yipping and howling.

Before that burning wolf even registered that he was burning alive and had fallen over, Lucas had used my magic once again to send a fireball in the direction of another wolf. More yipping from the remaining two reached my ears as I swiveled to launch a fireball at another wolf—the one I knew to be Jason. He was larger than the other four had been, so I knew that had to be him. As I raised my arm, Lucas' hand slipped from mine. I hadn't been paying attention when I had turned to aim at Jason, so I hadn't realized how loosely Lucas and I were holding onto each other.

As soon as my hand slipped from Lucas', and our connection to each other—his connection to a source of magic he could use to protect himself—slipped away, the Not Jason wolf jumped. I screamed out in horror as the wolf crashed into Lucas, and the two of them fell to the ground in a heap, the wolf on top of Lucas, its jaws snapping. Screaming out in rage, I turned back, intending to jump on the wolf that had leapt upon Lucas, knocking it away, but then my body was lifted off the ground. A bag of fur with four legs and snapping jaws followed me to the ground.

Jason came to rest on top of me as my back slammed into the hard earth of the garden, landing on all four of his paws. Disoriented and having had the breath knocked from my lungs, all I could do was grab wolf-Jason's neck and hold his head back as he attempted to snap at my face. Jason's glowing red eyes glared down at me as fangs snapped, and spittle dripped into my face. My hands couldn't even fit around his giant wolf neck, so choking him out wasn't an option. I could see the murderous look in his eyes, even though the eyes I was peering into weren't human. Lucas was screaming somewhere to my side, but I refused to turn my head to look for him, to see how he was doing, because it would have distracted me from protecting myself. I was no good to Lucas dead.

Wolf-Jason continued to snap his jaws, trying to get closer to my face as I screamed out in fear and rage and did my best to hold him back. While I never considered myself weak, my body wasn't at its best—and I was fighting a fucking wolf. Hardly any man is a match for a werewolf with human intelligence and preternatural strength. They'd have to be...

*Special.*

*I knew magic.*

*Fuck, I was dumb.*

*And so was Jason.*

My fear bled into my rage as I stopped screaming. I looked up into wolf-Jason's eyes angrily as I let my magic pour into my arms, down the length of them, and into my hands.

"Burn!" I growled, right before the fire burst from my palms.

Wolf-Jason was engulfed so quickly that I feared he might fall on me, trapping me beneath him, and sentence me to a fiery death as well. However, I couldn't even feel any heat from the fire, even as it burned away Jason's fur, and he leapt away, no longer trapping me beneath him. I watched just long enough to see him topple over onto his side, his legs kicking wildly, going nowhere, as he lay burning.

When I heard Lucas' screams again, the fury no longer impairing my focus, I leapt up from the ground and spun around, looking for Lucas and the wolf that had jumped on him. Less than a few yards away, Lucas was positioned in the same manner I had been with wolf-Jason on top of me. The last werewolf was standing over him, on all fours, effectively trapping him against the ground, snapping and snarling as Lucas did his best to push the beast's jaws away.

A few quick steps and my hand was against the side of the wolf as Lucas' hands stayed around its throat. The wolf had just enough time to glance at me out of the corner of its eye before I felt my magic rolling down my arm once again. Lucas looked up at me from the ground, relief flooding his face as I grinned evilly at the wolf I was about to kill.

"*And fuck you, too.*" I snapped.

Then the wolf burst into flames.

As I pulled Lucas to his feet, the wolf leaping away to collapse in a fiery ball, the first thing I noticed was the gash on Lucas' forehead, oozing viscous blood. Now that he had nothing to brace it against, his left arm hung limply at his side. Whether it was broken or dislocated, I had no idea, but something was definitely wrong with it. Fury rolled through me as Lucas stood there, bleeding and broken. I spun so that I could see all five burning heaps of wolf in the garden. With every ounce of energy I had in my body, and with my boyfriend bleeding and broken behind me, I summoned up my magic.

Sometimes, without being told, you just know some things to be true.

I knew that my eyes were glowing red.

Just like the wolves' eyes had.

Just like Bloody Bones.

Summoning every bit of rage I could, I focused that magic on the four burning heaps in the garden...and commanded my magic to do my bidding. Five different holes opened in the ground, swallowing the burning wolves, pulling them beneath the surface, dragging them down. Though I had no way of knowing for sure if they would end up where I wanted, I knew where I had told my magic to send them. And I hoped that my magic was powerful enough to do it. The holes in the ground were just beginning to fill back up, sealing away the wolves, the light from the fires being snuffed out, when I turned back to Lucas.

"Are you okay?" I asked, my eyes going to his.

Lucas looked...amazed.

"What did you do?" He asked, his good arm moving to cradle his hurt arm.

"Permanently solved a problem." I shrugged, stepping closer to him.

Lucas gave a brief smile, which was quickly replaced by a wince. I cringed and started to reach out to him. Unfortunately, as my body and arm moved as one, my eyes also moved. Black flashed in my vision, and my eyes were drawn over to the side of the garden fence where Bloody Bones now stood, his gleaming, bony smile and red eyes looking amused.

"Well done." He said as I stepped towards him, putting my body between him and Lucas. "Though I have to say, I am not shocked."

"You shouldn't be," I said as I felt Lucas' hand touch my shoulder for support. "You're next."

Bloody Bones' skull tilted back towards the heavens, and a long peal of laughter escaped his maw. In the corner of my eye, I could see Oma standing at her post, looking concerned. Obviously, no one had faith in what I had said.

"It's been eleven years since I've met a witch in battle." His coarse, gravelly voice met my ears. "I forgot how entertaining your kind can be."

"You want a show?" I snapped, my arm beginning to rise.

"I've learned from my mistakes in the past." Bloody Bones said. "And a few new tricks."

Before I could even blink, Bloody Bones' arm snapped up, and an orb of sickly green light burst forth. I didn't even have time to raise my arm. I certainly had no idea how to counter or block a spell. If I had a memory of being trained to do such a thing, it was failing me. All I had time to do was to realize that *this was it.* Maybe I had killed a few wolves...but I definitely was no match for Bloody Bones. Especially now that I didn't have a reservoir of magic the well had provided. I wasn't ready. And that was how I would die.

"***NO!***" Lucas screamed as magic flared in the air around us.

And then I was falling to the ground in a heap. The air was knocked from my lungs, and my vision blurred as a starless, moonless, black sky looked down on me. The world seemed to slow as my head swam from smacking against the ground so forcefully. Muffled sounds filled my ears.

*Did you see that?*

Shaking my head to clear the sounds and the confusion, I pushed off of the ground, rage filling me again as I came to my knees, my vision clearing, though I was still trying to catch my breath. Bloody Bones was still across from me at the garden fence...and he was smiling. Oma was standing a few yards away, a few feet within the fence perimeter, her mouth hung slack, her eyes wide and terrified.

All I could think was that, yes, Bloody Bones had knocked me on my ass...sent me reeling...but I was still alive.

But then I saw Lucas standing to my side. Looking up, I saw that he was looking down at his stomach, which he had his one good hand against. As I looked up, his head turned to me. His face was ashen, and a single tear was sliding down his cheek as his eyes met mine. Then he crumpled to his knees beside me. My voice caught in my throat as my face twisted in horror and disbelief when I saw the blood gushing out from between the fingers of the hand against his stomach.

My arms went out to catch Lucas as he fell into me, blood streaming down the front of him. Lucas' body was nearly dead weight in my arms as his body slumped against me, turning just enough so that he could look up at me, his face pasty white, his eyes looking dim, though they were wide open. His lips quivered, and his mouth opened as if to say something to me, but nothing came out, though another tear escaped his eye.

"Lucas." I gasped, holding him tightly, struggling to keep him off of the ground but also figure out what to do to help him.

Then Bloody Bones reeled back with an evil laugh, his arm held up aggressively. Another orb of sickly green light flew at us.

*And nothing happened.*

Bloody Bones jerked, and somehow, his skull-like face looked shocked.

*"I told him 'no.'"* Lucas croaked from his place in my arms, making me look back down at him.

Lucas' eyes searched my face as his blood oozed from his stomach and trickled between us, dripping onto my knees and the ground below. Reaching out with some part of my magic that was instinctive, something told me that there was nothing to be done. My boyfriend was dying right there in my arms as Oma watched—because that's what The Guardian does. It's what The Guardian has always done. And he had been killed by Bloody Bones. Because that's what Bloody Bones does. That's what he has always done. Tears welled in my eyes as I looked down at Lucas, trying to find the words to tell him how much I loved him. How sorry I was—*how everything in this moment was my fault and no one else's.*

Instead of my voice filling the space between us...faint green light did. And it wasn't coming from another offensive spell from Bloody Bones. It wasn't my magic. It was Lucas' eyes. They were glowing—like I had only seen them do once before. As if trying to communicate with me, and not having the use of his voice, Lucas' eyes searched my face, desperately trying to get me to understand something. For what seemed like hours, but was probably less than a second, I tried to understand what Lucas' eyes were telling me. Then, Lucas' fingers slithered across my forearm, smearing it with blood. Weaker than ever before, I felt Lucas draw my magic down my arm, almost like a trickle from a faucet...and his eyes glowed red.

A sudden realization went through me, and I gasped as I held my dying boyfriend.

*As above, so below.*

All things have to be equal.

And I was holding something that still contained part of Bloody Bones' stolen power. A piece that had refused to serve him. Someone who was going to die...*no matter what I did.* I could make things equal again. A tear slithered down my cheek as I looked down at Lucas in my arms, my lips slowly curling into a sad smile. Lucas somehow found the strength to give me a single nod, though no words escaped his lips.

"I love you," I said.

He nodded once more.

When I looked up from Lucas, my eyes settling on Bloody Bones, I knew that my eyes were glowing red once again. Underneath us all, the ground started to rumble and shake, and from the look that suddenly flooded Bloody Bones skull-like face, I knew that he knew someone else was the cause of it for once in his long life.

"Ohhhhhh, shit." I heard Oma crow, though I was too focused on the man made of bones in the black hooded cloak to search her out with my eyes. "You done pissed him off good, Red Eyes."

I want to say it was fury once again that filled me from the tips of my toes to the top of my head. But it wasn't. It wasn't a desire to make things equal due to altruism. It wasn't anger or rage.

*It was vengeance.*

*And that would have to be good enough.*

A howling scream emanated from my throat—a noise I never would have known I could make—as my head went back, and my face looked to the heavens. I drew all of the magic I could from my dying boyfriend, summoned up all of my own magic, and...

*I made a wish.*

The only wish that could make things right.

Put them back the way they ought to be.

The ground continued to shake as I screamed to the heavens, commanding anything that was listening to let me have my vengeance. A loud cracking sound filled the air, and the Earth split. Bloody Bones screamed in terror. When I stopped screaming to find him with my eyes, the ground was open beneath his feet, and what I could only describe as arms made of fire and melting flesh were pulling at him, dragging him down. A wicked grin split my face as my eyes continued to glow red, and I watched those...*things*...drag Bloody Bones into the ground.

Bloody Bones thrashed and fought, cast spells at the arm-like things attempting to drag him downwards, slowing their pull until he was no longer moving downward. In fact, he might have been reversing the pull, moving upwards infinitesimally. Desperately, I tried to search out more magic, trying to figure out what else I could put with my vengeance to finish the job...and my eyes landed on Oma. As soon as she saw that I had spotted her, standing by the fence, she rolled her eyes and sighed.

"Fine." She threw her hands up and began walking towards me and Lucas, who I couldn't bring myself to examine. "Ya' can't really create balance for good if you leave me behind, can ya'? Ain't got no damn oracle anyway."

My eyes met hers, and I smiled at her, unable to find words to say—not that my current state would have allowed me to speak eloquently. Bloody Bones saw Oma walking towards me and howled in rage, increasing his efforts to try and fight off the arms trying to pull him underneath. He fought harder and faster, but it didn't take Oma long enough to cross the distance between her and us. Coming to stand at my side, my shoulder even with her hip, she turned to face Bloody Bones as he struggled.

"Fuck you, Red Eyes." She cackled.

Then she placed her hand on my shoulder. I looked up at her.

"I only wish I'd eaten more donuts." I managed to say.

Oma continued to cackle as I smiled softly.

And I drew from her magic forcefully, grinning at Bloody Bones, looking him in the eyes as he was forcefully yanked down into the Earth by the arms that still held him. Fire shot from the crack in the ground, soaring into the sky in a pillar of fire as Bloody Bones' screams of agony descended further into the Earth until the sound of them could no longer reach my ears. Slowly, I crooked my head to look at Lucas. His eyes were closed, and I couldn't sense anything from him. Quickly, I crooked my neck to look up at Oma.

"Here comes the good part." She said, giving me a wink, though the smile on her face was sad.

I nodded at her, another tear rolling from my eye and over my cheek as I looked toward the house. The crack grew longer, reaching towards Oma, Lucas, and me. The three of us waiting for it to claim us as well. Just as the crack reached us, I saw movement at the corner of the house. Someone stumbling out of the decreasing shadows as the darkness dissolved from the sky, and the heralding dawn started to bathe the world in golden light once again.

*Andrew*?

Then the Earth was claiming the three of us.

# Chapter 14

"***NO!!!!***" Andrew screamed and pushed off from the side of the house, still out of breath from his journey from Main Street to Esther Jean Wagner's on foot—of which he now only had two.

Andrew raced across the yard, limping and skipping, the crack in the ground slowly inching shut, closing off the space where Esther Jean, Lucas, and Rob had disappeared. The sun slowly rose in the east as he awkwardly leapt the garden fence and dove towards the narrow crack in the garden, landing over it just as the last bit of Earth sealed shut. For the briefest of moments, the ground shook underneath, and then all was silent and still.

Rising to his knees, Andrew brought his hands to his head, a look of agony twisting his face as he gazed down at the Earth that was as smooth as it had been before this night. Bird song suddenly met his ears as the world came to life around him. A gentle, cold breeze blew in off of Lake Erie, over the trees, and greeted Andrew's back. Andrew looked around frantically, wondering if anyone else was around, wondering if there was someone who could help him figure out what to do. Esther Jean was gone. Carlita was dead. Mr. Barkley was probably dead. Everyone he had been working towards this moment with was…no more.

There was no one around to reach out to, to ask for help or guidance. Andrew didn't even have a pack to run off to in order to be consoled.

He was all alone in the backyard of a house that no longer had an owner and a garden that might never see planting again. With nothing more to do, Andrew pushed off of the ground in defeat and rose to his full height. Slowly, reaching up to wipe his nose with the back of his hand, Andrew turned on his heels. His feet began to move of his own accord as he walked towards the garden fence.

Barely at the perimeter of the garden, about to open the gate so that he could once again leave, find somewhere to go, someone to speak with, to help him forget this night, the ground shook briefly for another moment. Shocked and afraid, Andrew whipped around, expecting Bloody Bones to suddenly pop out of the ground.

But Bloody Bones did not suddenly appear out of the ground like he had on Main Street when the Earth had shaken. The ground didn't even crack. Instead, Andrew's eyes landed on a small green sprout that popped out of the ground like a thermometer on a roasted turkey. Andrew's eyes stayed on the sprout as it ever so slowly grew into a seedling. With ever-widening eyes, Andrew continued to watch as the seedling, nearly knee-high grew into a sapling. Though he didn't know why, Andrew began to smile as the sapling began to grow faster, picking up speed as its trunk widened, and its branches began to split and elongate, reaching towards the sky.

Bit by bit, the tree grew taller and broader as Andrew stood there in awe, backing up to give it room to grow without knocking him over. The trunk became wide than four men bundled together and the branches continued to split and thicken and reach into the sky. Then the process was complete. In under a minute, Andrew had been walking towards the garden fence, wondering what to do, and then he had watched a tiny sprout grow into a fully mature tree. One that would have taken decades—if not centuries—to grow.

Andrew looked up at the tree in wonder, examining its thick bark and gnarly roots that surely anchored it securely and deeply into the Earth. Hundreds of branches adorned the massive tree that towered over him in the garden, reaching out in an umbrella of brownish-black over Andrew's head. He continued to stare in awe as his eyes were drawn to one of the lower branches that seemed to shiver against the cool breeze coming off of the lake. Before his very eyes, a single bud appeared from a knot in the tree branch, slowly unfurling to show that the tree was announcing the coming Spring.

Smiling to himself, Andrew's eyes closed languidly. He sniffed the air, hoping he would smell Esther Jean, Lucas, or Rob on the air...but all he smelled was fresh air and dirt. Frowning to himself, Andrew wondered why his keen senses from being a werewolf did not pick up anything else...just as they always had. His eyes grew wide as an idea struck him. As he had done, many thousands of times before, Andrew willed himself into wolf form.

And nothing happened.

He was still human-Andrew, standing before a tree that hadn't existed just minutes before.

There was nothing for Andrew to do but smile and say his thanks as the warm, golden light of the sun kissed his skin.

It was the first time he'd ever had to thank a witch.

*"Thanks, Tom!" The field reporter spoke into her microphone as she looked into the camera.*

*Behind her, the smoke and wreckage of Main Street created a harrowing scene with which to frame her story. Plumes of blackish, sooty smoke rose from Barkley's Hardware Store. The firefighters were still putting out small clusters of fire that were still burning in the First National Bank of Point Worth. The Sunny Side-Up Café was nothing but rubble. Men—naked for some reason—lay in the middle of the street, badly battered and bruised. A crack ran down the center of Main Street, nothing but darkness and cold below. A woman, partially covered by a sheet, was lying in the street, her heels with red soles sticking out from the bottom. The reporter gestured towards the scene behind her.*

*"As you can see behind me here, Tom, and our viewers at home," She waved, shaking her head sadly, "the town of Point Worth, a small community within walking distance of the shores of Lake Erie, is in ruins. No one knows what caused these fires or many of these buildings to collapse, or what happened to these poor people behind me. The police are canvassing the town as we speak, looking for any citizen of Point Worth who might be able to shed some light on what happened in this little berg. The anonymous person who called the Toledo Police Department this morning merely said that there were problems in Point Worth, but failed to elaborate, give a name,*

*or even stay on the line long enough for the dispatchers to thoroughly question him.*

*"What we do know is that whatever happened here could possibly happen anywhere in this great state of ours. That is why the police are trying to put the pieces together and find anyone who might be able to let them know what happened. It's in all Ohioans' best interest to know if this was an isolated incident, or maybe even an act of terror. But—"*

# Chapter 15

"Did you see that?"

Rolling my eyes, I paused, stopping my pitch to look across the table. Three faces were huddled over the scripts I had provided at the beginning of the meeting, pointing and jabbing at the pages before them. Of course, I could've ignored yet another irritating statement in the middle of my pitch, but I was about done being polite with these three morons. Placing my hands on top of the table, I laced my fingers and stared at the people across from me. Letting a smile form on my face, I waited for them to notice I had stopped speaking.

"Did you see that?" The man on the right—Bob, I think—tapped his script again. "Right there. He wants to kill every damn character in this thing!"

"Thanks for the spoiler alert." The lady in the middle—Lucinda, I believe—rolled her eyes.

I liked her.

"Someone has to die, right?" The man on the other side of Lucinda shrugged.

His name was Ron. I had worked with him before.

"You can't really have this type of story and expect it to have a fairytale ending," Ron added.

"Why not?" Bob snipped. "Everyone loves a happy ending."

"Do they?" Lucinda gave him a saccharine sweet smile. "Do they really, Bob? People bitched for weeks and weeks about each death on *Game of Thrones,* but they kept tuning in, didn't they?"

"That's different!" Bob proclaimed.

"How?" Ron backed Lucinda up.

"They didn't kill the whole goddamn cast in one episode!"

"They killed *a lot of the cast* in single episodes. *The Red Wedding,* for example." Lucinda gestured vaguely. "You have had an issue on nearly every damn page of this script."

"This isn't *Game of Thrones*!" Bob added angrily.

"Bob, just look at it this way." Ron tried to play peacemaker. "If we—"

Before either Lucinda or Ron could stop him, Bob growled with frustration and pushed away from the table. My eyes tracked his movements as he jumped up from his chair and marched toward the door to the conference room, his chair still spinning lazily from the exertion. Once the door to the conference room had slammed shut behind him, I let my head turn back to Lucinda and Ron. They both looked apologetic—and frankly, embarrassed for their partner.

"Sorry." Lucinda winced.

"Don't apologize for a man." I raised an eyebrow. "Especially one like Bob."

Ron laughed as Lucinda let a smile come back to her face—we were obviously going to be friends. "This ain't your first rodeo with Bob, is it, Jacob?"

I shrugged.

"We have his opinion," I said, gesturing at the three scripts still open on the other side of the table. "What do you think of *Jacob Michaels Is...*?

Think we can send it to series? Get the green light to at least fund a pilot?"

Lucinda chewed at her lip thoughtfully as Ron glanced over at her.

"Jacob." He sighed.

"Yes?"

"It is very dark. And everyone *does* die at the end." He gave me an apologetic look. "And, I mean, the Oma character. Love her, don't get me wrong. But this isn't going on network. We'd have to change her whole personality if we pitched to network. You know that, right?"

I laughed.

"Andrew didn't die," I said. "And I was thinking premium or Netflix."

"No one's going to give a shit about Andrew." Lucinda chuckled, though I could tell she hated breaking that news. "I mean, he's not a sympathetic character. He's kind of like the Severus Snape."

"Without a really good backstory." Ron helped her.

"Oma and Lucas." Lucinda brightened. "Those are your fan favorites. And you butchered one and sacrificed the other."

"Lucas and Oma?" I chuckled. I wasn't offended. "Rob gets no love, huh?"

They both laughed.

"Carlita." Ron performed a 'chef's kiss' type motion. "People will die for her. But you killed her off as well. Hell, even Lucas' grandfather got axed. In fact, it's pretty clear that most everyone in the town died—even ones you'd never know about. You left the one character no one will feel all that sympathetic towards. I mean...we live in the age of the internet, Jacob. They'll absolutely roast your ass on Twitter."

"I live to be dragged on Twitter." I shrugged.

Lucinda and Ron exchanged a look.

"Ron," I chuckled warmly, doing my best 'Nice Jacob Michaels' impersonation, "have I brought you anything that turned out to be bad before? Every movie we've worked on together has done well enough. Some have even done really well. Not a single stinker in the bunch."

Lucinda and Ron seemed to decide something telepathically, so Lucinda turned to me to speak whatever it was they had discussed subliminally.

"Jacob," She said, "this is very meta. It's cool. I mean, you're *Jacob Michaels*, your real name is Robert Wagner, and you're from Ohio, and you want to make a series where an actor with the stage name 'Jacob Michaels' goes home to Ohio to get away from the toxicity of Hollywood. I love that. But..."

"But what?"

"People might start to think this is really your life story," Ron explained.

"They'll think I really grew up in a house with a magical old lady and tiny little creatures that did household chores, and my hometown was full of people with magical abilities and werewolves? That I can shoot lasers and fire from my hands? That's crazy." I couldn't help but let a laugh escape my mouth.

Both Ron and Lucinda turned a pinkish color, but they laughed with me.

"Well, okay." Ron held his hands up. "Who do you see in the supporting roles? I mean...it sounds like..."

"Yeah." I nodded, stopping him. "Obviously Esther Jean Wagner for Oma. Lucas Barkley for

Lucas Barkley...I found some new talent for Jason, Carlita, and Andrew, and—"

"You want your real grandmother and boyfriend to play your grandmother and boyfriend—and you want the characters to have the same names as the real people?" Lucinda's brow furrowed, thinking this over.

"Yeah." I shrugged as if this was the most natural thing in the world.

"Jacob." Ron gave a barking laugh. "Lucas has barely even managed to land supporting roles in the past...and now you want to give him a role in a project like this?"

"Talk about nepotism," Lucinda spoke out of the corner of her mouth to Ron.

They both laughed, but it wasn't at my expense.

"Sure." I shrugged. "He can do it. You said meta is good, right?"

"I just said it was cool. Not good." Lucinda teased.

"And your grandmother—God love her—" Ron began, "she's an incredible actress. But how long has it been since she's acted? The 70s?"

"She did some T.V. and a few movies in the 80s and 90s." I corrected him, though I knew he knew those things.

"Pardon me." He laughed.

"Come on, guys." I rolled my eyes with a smile, trying to be affable. "Jacob Michaels, his legendary actress grandmother—"

'That's pushing it." Lucinda mumbled.

"—his actor boyfriend. All from Ohio. All playing themselves in a T.V. show that pretends to be about their real life. It's like reality T.V. meets situational comedy meets dramedy. And it's full of magic and fantasy in my hometown in

Ohio. Don't tell me people wouldn't eat that shit up if we do it right. People are dying for LGBTQ plus representation in their media. They want to see meaty roles for older women. Everyone loves drag queens—even Republicans. We could easily show the juxtaposition between the glamour of Hollywood and regular working-class Americans. It would be easy to show social issues and discuss them visually. But in a heightened reality, fantasy way that appeals to a broader audience than those just looking for something real. It's the best of both worlds. You could appeal to people out here and people in middle America. This is one of those shows that easily trends on social media every Sunday night and is discussed in workplaces across American on Monday. And the Kobolds? Ernst? Think of the action figures and stuffed dolls possibility. So…much…merch."

Again, Lucinda and Ron exchanged looks, seemed to have a telepathic discussion, and agreed on something quietly.

"We're not denying that it's intriguing—" Ron began.

"You, your grandmother, and Lucas are not getting paid well first season. Maybe the first two." Lucinda interjected.

"My feelings." I held a hand to my heart with a smile. "So…are we going to work on developing this?"

Another look between the two.

"Fine." Ron sighed.

"Don't sound too happy." I teased as I rose from my seat.

"I just don't know where we'll find little people to play the Kobolds." Ron ruminated. "I mean, there's always CGI, but that's expensive. Maybe forced perspective will work…"

“It’s going to be a tough sell,” Lucinda added a sigh and stood.

“I have a very inexpensive solution.” I smiled warmly. “Don’t worry.”

“I guess we’ll see what the studios say.” Ron shrugged with a laugh.

“I have a feeling that when you take it to streaming, one of them will snatch it up. Easy three-seasons green light.” I held a hand out towards her. “And then you can apologize for that comment.”

Lucinda and Ron laughed, but ultimately, we all shook hands.

Then I was leaving the production office.

The drive out to Calabasas is too long when there’s good news to be shared. It was a sunny day, though there is never a shortage of such a thing in southern California. For the first time in my life as a celebrity, I wished that I didn’t have a Lincoln MKZ but something sportier, something the roof could be lowered on. Maybe a BMW 4 Series or a Corvette…hell, even a Jeep Wrangler would have been nice on such a wonderful day. To feel the sun on my face and neck and arms as I drove from the production office meeting back home, the wind whipping through my hair as *Scissor Sisters* blared from the radio would have made it the best day it possibly could have been.

Lucinda and Ron had been skeptical—or, more accurately, they had pretended to be skeptical—but they were going to help develop *Jacob Michaels Is...* into something we could sell to Netflix or Hulu. Maybe even Amazon Prime. Then, Oma, Lucas, and I would find ourselves on a studio lot—maybe even on location—shooting our first ever project as a family and team. I couldn't have been happier. Of course, I worked enough for all of us, there was no lack of money coming into our household, but I knew how desperately Oma wanted to get back to work on something substantial. Having a starring—or even co-starring—role in anything would make Lucas so happy. He had never been given a chance to show what a talented actor he was.

When I pulled into the driveway at home, easing the car into the garage next to Lucas' old pickup truck that had come with us from Point Worth a decade prior, I smiled. Oma's old Cadillac was on the far end of the garage, nearly permanently parked there since she always had someone to drive her anywhere. It was almost like yesterday that Oma had convinced the two of us two travel out to Hollywood to "give this acting thing a shot." Now...here we were...living in Calabasas, living the dream, and about to star in our first project as a family. Life couldn't possibly get better.

The garage closed quietly behind me as I entered the house. I didn't bother hollering out, trying to figure out where everyone was. Oma and Lucas had to be in the same place they always were when they had the day off. They'd both been waiting for me to get home from my meeting to tell them the outcome. I walked through the house, all floor-to-ceiling windows, granite, and steel, making my way to the back patio. Just as I had suspected, as I looked out through the glass doors that looked out over the patio, I saw Lucas and Oma seated at the table. Lucas had his nose in a book with a glass of lemonade on the table before him. Oma was staring out at the hills, a flute of champagne in her hand, held grandly before her. It was a nice contrast to the house dress and slippers she hadn't changed out of since breakfast.

Before I could make my way out to the patio to be with my boyfriend and grandmother, I felt my phone vibrate in my pocket. I extracted my phone, tapped the screen, and glanced down at the text message I'd received:

> **Ron: How about more of a murder mystery with fantasy or paranormal elements? We won't touch the characters or give you shit about who plays which character.**

Smiling widely to myself, I realized that the script had hooked Ron and Lucinda more than they had been willing to let on in the meeting. No producer ever messaged so quickly after a pitch meeting. Quickly, but not so quickly as to seem desperate, I tapped out my short response.

*Deal.*

As I stepped out onto the patio, Oma turned her head to look at me, raising her champagne flute in a salute with a smile.

"Afternoon, assface." She quipped before bringing her drink to her lips.

"Good afternoon, you old bag." I nudged her shoulder with my hip as I went by. "How's the sauce?"

"Well," She sighed and smacked her lips, "I've had worse."

I laughed as I slid into the seat next to Lucas, who still had his nose in his book. A quick glance at the cover let me know that he was rereading *Interview with the Vampire* by Anne Rice. Using my forefinger, I thumped the cover, and Lucas jerked in his seat. Looking up from his book, as though he had been somewhere else entirely, he looked over the top of the book. For a second, he seemed disoriented, then his eyes met mine, and a smile bloomed on his face.

"Babe." He stated happily.

"Research?" I asked, nodding at the book.

Lucas set his book on the patio table, spine up, and leaned forward to give me a chaste, yet lingering kiss.

"Mmm." I winked as he pulled away.

"Not really research," He gestured at the book, "but, just in case they didn't like what you took to them today, maybe I could be inspired to come up with a better idea to tweak what we wrote."

"They liked it." I leaned in with a grin.

Lucas' eyes grew wide with joyful surprise, and his lips were on mine once again.

"Well, good," Oma grumbled from the other side of the table. "Y'all didn't have enough reasons to swap spit, did ya'?"

"Can it, old woman." I teased her as Lucas' arms went around my neck, giving me a celebratory hug. "This is good news."

"Yeah?" She turned in her seat to look at us as Lucas' arms slid from my neck, and he beamed at me. “Betcha dollars to donuts them sumbitches loved the idea of you in the lead, but where does that leave me and handsome over there?”

“Thank you, Mrs. Wagner.” Lucas laughed.

“They probably told you that ‘the old hag’ and your ‘boy toy’ had to sit this one out, didn’t they?” Oma waggled her head and slammed the rest of her champagne.

“I don’t like that nickname nearly as much.” Lucas turned up his nose.

“Ignore her.” I patted his knee. “As a matter of fact, Oma, they are on board with all three of us. They said they want to change it to a murder mystery with paranormal and fantasy elements, but otherwise, they’re going to move forward with all three of us.”

Oma’s brow raised.

“Well,” The corner of her mouth turned up, “didn’t think you had it in you to make that kind of deal. The washed-up old has-been and the professional extra get called up to the big leagues.”

Lucas frowned at her, but he wasn’t wholly unamused.

“Stuff it, Oma.” I did my best not to chuckle.

“Oh, boy. It’s true what they say. You don’t buy champagne, ya’ rent it.” Oma stated simply before rising from her chair and scuttling toward the house.

Lucas watched her go, shaking his head amusedly.

“We should probably celebrate.” He finally said once Oma was out of earshot. “Do you want to go out?”

"You hate going out." I leaned in with a grin and laid my forehead against his.

"I do."

"Maybe you'll be saying that phrase in a different context in the future?" I wiggled my eyebrows.

"Ya' never know." He winked.

"Time will tell." I sighed happily.

"I'll make us something special for dinner. Lots of wine." He slowly rose from his chair, so I sat back in mine to give him space. "Then, when the old lady goes to bed, we'll do disrespectful things."

"Obscenely disrespectful." I winked up at him.

Lucas grinned wickedly and made his way toward the house, just like Oma had. Of course, unlike Oma, he most likely wasn't going to the fridge to attack the champagne after visiting the bathroom. I sat back in the patio chair and propped my elbows on the table, smiling to myself. Just thinking about developing a project with the two people I loved most in life would keep me happy for a long time. Unless things fell through, and the project just couldn't be brought to the small screen, I knew that I would be even happier in the months to come.

I nearly jumped out of my skin as a hand suddenly found my knee and had to stop myself from screaming out. Holding a hand to my chest, I laughed as the small man crept out from under the table. Ernst gave me an apologetic smile as he patted my knee and came to stand beside me.

"*I don' like California, Rob.*" He said in his high-pitched voice. "*Too much sun. I like shadows.*"

He squinted and held a hand over his eyes to block out some of the sunlight that threatened his senses.

I laid a hand on his shoulder. "I know. The others have said the same thing. Give it time. In a few months, maybe we'll all be back in Ohio."

Ernst's eyes lit up from underneath the visor made of his hand.

"*Did they like your ideas*?" He asked, hopefully.

"They did." I smiled down at him.

"*We've been 'ere so long.*" He sighed. "*I woul' love to be back 'ome.*"

I patted his shoulder and gave it a squeeze as I looked out at the sunlit hills around us.

"We'll see what the future brings, my friend." I smiled. "Only time will tell. Have faith."

And…scene.

# About the Author

Chase Connor currently lives in Des Moines, Iowa with his dog, Rimbaud, and spends his free time writing M/M Romance, LGBTQ YA novellas/novels, LGBTQ Paranormal Romance, as well as general LGBTQ fiction, when he's not busy being enthusiastic about naps and Pad Thai.

Chase can be reached at
chaseconnor@chaseconnor.com
Or on Twitter @ChaseConnor7
He can also be found on Chase Connor Books
https://chaseconnor.com
(New blog posts every second and fourth Tuesday of each month)

He does his very best to respond to all DMs, emails, and Twitter comments from his reader friends and loves the interaction with them. Chase has several novellas/novels for sale on Amazon (and other sites) in ebook and paperback format.

***Most of Chase Connor's catalog can be read for FREE on Kindle Unlimited***

**Expected Future Releases from Chase Connor**

*A BOY CALLED NEVER*
*A MILLION LITTLE SOULS*
*IT MEANS SOMETHING DIFFERENT*
*ONE BRICK KINGDOM*
*VISITING MUSEUMS WITH PETRUCHIO*
*SOMETIMES THE RAIN ANSWERS*
*SENDING LOVE LETTERS TO ANIMALS: AND OTHER TOTALLY NORMAL HUMAN BEHAVIORS*
*WHEN WORDS GROW FANGS*
*THE WARMTH OF OUR CLOSEST STAR*

**And**

*A POINT WORTH LGBTQ PARANORMAL ROMANCE – BOOKS 7, 8, & 9*

www.ingramcontent.com/pod-product-compliance
Lightning Source LLC
Chambersburg PA
CBHW020346180626
46812CB00001B/365

* 9 7 8 1 9 5 1 8 6 0 0 4 2 *